WINGS OF A NIGHTINGALE

It's 1941 when strong-willed Aussie nurse, Pauline Newton, arrives at Killymoor Hall, a British military hospital which has many secrets. Most crucially, it's a base for a team of Nazi saboteurs. Falling in love with the mysterious Sergeant Ray Tennyson, Pauline finds herself involved in murders, skulduggery and intrigue as they both race desperately to discover the German leaders' identity. Throughout it all, Ray and Pauline must resolve their own differences if they hope to stop the Nazis altering the War's outcome forever.

ALAN C. WILLIAMS

WINGS OF A NIGHTINGALE

Complete and Unabridged

LINFORD
Leicester

First published in Great Britain in 2020

First Linford Edition
published 2021

A catalogue record for this book is available
from the British Library.

ISBN 978–1–4448–4679–9

Published by
Ulverscroft Limited
Anstey, Leicestershire

Set by Words & Graphics Ltd.
Anstey, Leicestershire
Printed and bound in Great Britain by
TJ Books Ltd., Padstow, Cornwall
This book is printed on acid-free paper

1

'Get a move on!' the bolshie girl said as I gathered my possessions from the luggage rack above my seat. I glared at her then resumed lifting my bag down, saying nothing. There was always one, someone with the belief she was better than the rest of us nurses on the bus. She was from Melbourne judging by her accent. They called a castle, 'castle' whereas we New South Welsh people made it sound like 'carstle'.

There was a rivalry between the two states even now, in the middle of the war. The fact she'd called me a 'cockie' was a reference to me being from the country. Farmers had a problem with galahs and cockatoos eating the wheat seed, having learned to open the grain sacks with their beaks. The name stuck and now anyone from outside the big smoke was a cockie. Even nurses like me, born and bred in a decent-sized town.

Brenda was becoming impatient. She shoved me so I dropped the heavy bag on her foot, accidental-like then picked it up and left her hopping around in the aisle.

'Get a move on, ladies,' the elderly bus driver called out It was pouring outside and wasn't going to let up soon. 'Welcome to Killymoor Hall. It'll be your new home . . . for awhiles anyhow.'

I was glad to stretch my legs at last. The trip seemed to have taken ages which was weird considering the size of Britain compared to Australia. The last half-hour had been the worst; after dusk fell, the driver had to negotiate the narrow country lanes more by feel than by sight. We understood the reason, of course; the headlamps were virtually blacked out to avoid showing our lights and position to the German bombers overhead on their frequent raids.

'Serves Brenda right,' whispered Nancy in my ear. Nancy had also suffered the barbs of Brenda's spiteful loud mouth. Although she was from Canberra, she had been called a cockie also. Brenda had declared her feelings loudly early on the trip that it wasn't right for 'proper civilized women' like her to be cooped up with so many country bumpkins or, as she so eloquently put it, 'a flock of flaming galahs'.

Of course, she quietened down when Little Lois, who normally wouldn't say boo to a goose, stood up and reminded Big-Mouth Brenda that a galah's beak can give anyone who ignored them a pretty nasty bite. It was the most any of us had heard Lois say in all the weeks we'd known her.

I reckoned Brenda got the message for a while at least. Lois was a tall girl. She was five feet eleven and built like a brick dunny but you couldn't meet a kinder, more polite person. If Brenda had riled her, then she'd made an enemy for life. Lois didn't forgive or forget easily.

'Thank you,' I said to the driver as I clambered down the steps. Nancy was behind me.

'You're more than welcome. Miss,' he replied. I hadn't heard any other nurse speak to him as they disembarked. Too tired, I guessed.

Then he added some words that reminded me how much most English people appreciated their colonial cousins helping out.

'It's great to have you over here, helping look after our injured Tommies. You're all angels.'

I held a raincoat over my head as I made a dash for it, the other hand holding my case. Our larger bags would be unloaded and brought in later. It was comforting that we were all being cared for, in recognition of our roles here with the sick and wounded soldiers, sailors and airmen.

The war had been going on far too long and yet there wasn't an end in sight. At least there was talk of the Yanks possibly joining us. Some said 'not before time' but I was more philosophical about it than that. After all, this conflict had started in Europe, twelve thousand miles from us Aussies and there were plenty of people who reckoned it wasn't Australia's war either. Nonetheless, here I was along with thousands of diggers because Australia was part of the Empire and we owed it to Britain to do our bit.

Nancy skidded and almost fell as we ran across the cobbles to the grand staircase outside the former Manor House.

'Careful, chook,' I called out, letting her link her arm in mine. Why she insisted on wearing high heels all the time was beyond me.

Some soldiers were shining torches to guide us up the precarious steps to the double doors at the top. They were listening carefully for any sounds of aircraft but, given the poor visibility, I thought any self-respecting Luftwaffe Heinkels and Junkers were probably busy elsewhere raining destruction onto civilians.

Although we weren't supposed to realise it, there was a Royal Ordinance Factory near Chorley not far away and so there was a possibility that it was a prime target and we all were mindful that the bombers often missed their targets. We were a hospital yet those Germans wouldn't be aware of that and if they did, they or at least their superiors wouldn't care.

We reached the relatively dry and warmth of the Hall, stopping in the wide entrance area to put our belongings on the tiled floor. Matron and some Captain, from his insignia, were waiting impatiently, Matron glaring sternly at us, arms crossed across her ample bosom. The Captain was in full uniform even down to his cap.

As the last woman arrived and the door was closed, the head nurse introduced herself as Matron Jones or, her preferred sobriquet, simply Matron. The Captain was a doctor, in charge of the medical aspects of the hospital. Matron then chose to do a roll-call. It was evident from her lilting accent that she was Welsh whilst the eight of us were all Aussies. Well, almost all. Ruth who was a Kiwi. She was still okay, though.

We stood there patiently, dripping onto the marble tiled floor. The echoes of her voice reverberated off the walls giving it an almost auditorium feel. I examined the vast room with miniature eagles guarding the sweeping staircase that seemed to rise up to heaven.

'Golly,' I muttered under my breath. Matron must have had ears like a bat.

'Something you would care to share with us, Nurse . . . ?'

'Newton, Matron. Pauline Newton. I was just remarking on this place. It's . . . impressive.'

Matron glared down at me. She was standing three stairs up to avoid being looked down upon by most of us. I reckoned she was five foot high. Most of us were a good six inches taller. 'We don't bother with Christian names so much here, Nurse Newton. I run a tight ship and familiarity detracts us from our task here; to care for sick and injured military personnel. As for using Killymoor Hall, the owners kindly allow us to use their property as a hospital and rehabilitation unit. It is, as you so quaintly say, 'impressive' and it behoves us . . . all of us, to respect that. Cleanliness is next to Godliness and is necessary to maintain a hygienic environment for our charges. To that end, you will all be expected to help in the cleaning. There will be no exceptions.'

I suspected the property's owners hadn't had much say in the acquisition of Killymoor Hall. Nevertheless, I was glad we were here rather than in some derelict, leaky barn. We shifted uncomfortably under Matron Jones' officious scrutiny. Sensing that perhaps, she dropped her hands to her sides.

'I do realise that you are all from the colonies and as such may have different standards to those of British nurses and my good self. I'm certain, however, that we will make an efficient and caring team, just as long as you follow my instructions without question. You will be taken through to the former servants' quarters and allowed to familiarise yourselves with your accommodation tonight. Following that, you will eat in your quarters. Cook has been asked to prepare a hot evening meal for you all tonight. It goes without saying that there will be absolutely no fraternisation with the gentlemen, be they patients, civilians, military personnel or doctors. We're at war, ladies. Never forget that.'

She nodded to the Captain who, I suspected, was also intimidated by her overbearing attitude. He was leaning on a cane.

Matron Jones continued, 'I want you all on duty, fully dressed in your uniforms and ready to commence duties at 6am. Breakfast will be served at 5.15. One final thing. I will need to appoint a Sister from among you.' I saw Brenda raise her eyes from her shoes, suddenly attentive.

'Nurse Newton. You have more than one year's experience in the field. Tobruk and Greece I believe, from your service records. I've made the necessary applications to your superiors and you will commence duties tomorrow. Whilst I realise this is far from standard protocol, we are in desperate times.'

Brenda was impatient to speak up. 'Excuse me, Matron. My name is Nurse Isherwood. I'm the natural choice for the position of Sister. I'm older than Nurse Newton and I've been nursing longer.' Her tone was belligerent and confrontational.

Matron gave a broad grin before moving down the stairs and across the floor to Brenda. She was far shorter yet exuded a confidence and power that I had rarely witnessed. She faced Brenda, her neck bent upward to better address the blond-headed Victorian.

'Obviously you are new here, Nurse Isherwood and may not have been listening earlier. This is not a democracy and you have no right to question my decisions. Not that I owe you any explanation, young lady, but I will give you one. Purely because I am a kind woman who wishes to be friends with you. Would you like me to tell you and all of your colleagues the reasons I dismissed you as my choice? Think carefully. I have studied all of the group's service records. Especially yours.'

Matron's tone was subdued, her voice calm. I suspected she was like a sleeping lioness being taunted by a particularly stupid hyena, only prepared to tolerate the annoying pest so much.

Brenda, being Brenda, failed to appreciate her adversary's power.

'Yes, Matron. By all means, let's hear the explanation for your stupid decision,' she said.

Nancy and I repressed our sniggers when Matron's eyes flashed a peek in our direction.

'Very well. But remember this, Nurse Brenda Isherwood. It was you who asked for it. Nurse Newton has served with distinction in Alexandria, Malta and the Greek Islands. Her superiors' reports of her skills in combat situations far exceed those of most nurses that I've met.'

Then Matron Jones turned back to Brenda, their faces inches apart. 'That you are older and have served as a nurse for longer is undeniable. You, on the other hand, Nurse Isherwood, have had no combat hospital experience having only arrived from Melbourne two weeks ago. During your time there, you were on a children's ward dealing mainly with non-urgent cases. There were those suffering from polio and TB but your involvements revolved mainly around colic and sun-burn. The most positive comment one Sister made about you some months ago was that, and I quote, 'Nurse Isherwood's colouring-in skills are second to none'.' By this time, Brenda had backed away, her face the same colour as our Aussie nursing capes.

'Matron. Please don't go on. I'm sorry I questioned your choice.'

Matron moved forward, keeping her chubby face close to Brenda's.

'Not go on? What a shame. There is so much more. That means I won't be able to tell all of your friends about the reason for your transfer to here in England and now Killymoor Hall.'

Brenda's attempts to shush our Matron were being ignored. Finally, she sat down in a heap on the floor and stared upwards at her tormentor.

Matron could have left it at that but she didn't. She had a point to make. 'Nurse Isherwood. You are not suitable for a role as Sister under my supervision and I'm surprised that you believed that I would even consider it. Even Trainee Nurse Xavier has more integrity than you. You had an affair with a married doctor at your hospital. If his wife hadn't discovered your tryst and told her father, the Hospital Director, you'd still be there in St Vincent's . . . 'colouring in'.'

Matron turned her back on the hapless victim, who now was crying uncontrollably.

'Nurse Isherwood. You are on sluice duty for the next week. Never question my decisions again. Is that clear?'

In between sobs, we heard a very contrite, 'Yes, Matron.'

It was a valuable lesson for us all. I was going to decline Matron's 'invitation' to be promoted to Sister and, had Brenda not spoken up, I would have. Now, I simply wasn't game to do so. Life here would be hard enough without exacerbating the situation with my new boss. On reflection, I might enjoy the challenge. There was no doubt in my mind that I could handle the tasks afforded by this new role. I'd done most of the additional responsibilities already in Europe and Africa, in conditions far more hazardous than here.

The trials would still be there, caring for the wounded and sick, yet we'd not have the added pressures of severe supply shortages, last-minute evacuations or being torpedoed at sea. A semblance of stability in this chaotic world of death and destruction would

14

be a welcome change for this Wagga Wagga girl.

The others had left, following some elderly corporal, presumably to our future digs. Only Nancy and I were left behind with Brenda.

'Come on,' I said holding out a hand to the bereft woman. Instead of gratitude, I received a spiteful glare.

'Clear off, Sister Cockie. This is all your fault. Yours.' With that, she struggled to her feet in a very undignified way and traipsed off after the others. Nancy and I swapped glances, shrugged our shoulders and followed. Life in Killymoor Hall would certainly not be a cake-walk.

★ ★ ★

Dinner was a simple affair, one that Brenda again found cause about which to complain.

'What's this garbage?'

'Powdered egg,' some other nurse said.

'And this? Looks like meat but smells like horse manure. Where's my steak?' She had quite a shrill voice on her, one that grated on my nerves like when Miss Christie wrote on the blackboard with chalk in primary school.

'It's called Spam. Get used to it, Brenda. As for steak, forget it. England's on rations or didn't you notice?' It was the same nurse, Hilda or Hillary. Clearly, none of the others thought much of Brenda, more so after the revelation that she was an adulteress. Those who were married were quietly afraid of their hubbies back in Oz, being seduced by a Jezebel exactly like Brenda.

'Rations? That little book I was given when I arrived in this backward country?' She fished it out of a pocket in her cardie. We'd all worn civvies on the bus trip up here. 'According to this, I'm entitled to four ounces of cheese today. See here,' she remonstrated, thrusting the booklet in front of Cook's nose.

We were on the same rations as Army

personnel and I was aware that ordinary cheese rations were three ounces unless you were vegetarian or possibly pregnant.

Cook snatched the book from Brenda's hand. 'You shouldn't have this young lady. I'm in charge of ordering food for everyone and making certain you get equal shares.'

'But it's mine,' Brenda protested.

'Not any longer.' Cook surveyed the rest of us tucking in. 'Anyone else holding out? No. Good. And by the way, Miss Shirley hoity-toity Temple, that four ounces of cheese in your book is for a week . . . not a day.'

Once again, Brenda had humiliated herself. When would she learn when to close that cake-hole of hers? She resumed eating, deciding, at last, that it was time to keep a low profile.

However, the damage was done. Already I could hear whispers from those down the end of the long wooden table. The word 'Shirley' was distinct. I suspected it would be Brenda's nickname from now on. The fleeting observation by Cook, comparing Brenda's tight ringlets to the Yank film-star was now to be a part of Brenda's life in Killymoor Hall, whether she liked it or not.

Matron Jones came in after tea to check we were settling in. She told us that we'd all be working together, the British nurses working other shifts. As expected, I was given separate accommodation well away from my charges. Even I realised they needed private time away from the constant supervision of their superiors. I wouldn't be their friend any longer. I couldn't be. Nancy and I would be the exception. We'd been together for fifteen months now. I trusted her with my life. Nonetheless, I couldn't show any favouritism to her, a fact she was already well aware of.

In my private bedroom, I was arranging my grey serge dress on my bed. The red cape, white detachable collar and headdress were ready, the starched fabric comfortingly crisp to the touch. I was proud to be a member of the Australian Army Nursing Service. We even had our own Rising Sun badge; silver instead of the brass ones worn by the men. It said Australian Imperial Forces, A.I.F. We nurses wore it at the base of the neck, pinned to our capes. Matron knocked on the closed door before entering. I'd expected this visit.

'Pauline? May I call you by your first name?' she began. I was surprised by the familiarity. Most women of her age used surnames only.

'Of course,' I replied.

'I'm Blodwyn. I tend to be a tad . . . unconventional in my approach. It's this damn war. If you follow all the rules, nothing happens so I tend to be a little different. You colonials are only here because I kicked up a fuss about lack of nurses. They keep sending us the wounded, expecting miracles. My nurses were dead on their feet.'

That explained it. We were heading back Down Under when we were posted here in Lancashire. Although I would have preferred to help our blokes back home, I went where they sent me.

We chatted about procedures, plans and the challenges of this makeshift hospital. She'd produced a bottle of brandy to toast our future professional relationship. Not too much. After all, I had more responsibilities now and it was getting late. As I was walking Matron out past the nurses' accommodation, we were both feeling pretty relaxed and positive about the changes.

Suddenly there was a strange light from outside filtering through the blackout curtains. We both noticed it, as did some of the nurses. Before we could investigate, a tremendous explosion shook the ancient home to its foundations. I heard a glass window shatter nearby.

'What the dickens?' I shouted, steadying myself from the shock. As one, we rushed to the windows, pulling the black heavy material to peer outside. It was in the distance, perhaps five miles away on the flat horizon.

Even the heavy rain couldn't disguise the devastation and fireball that now dominated the area between the trees.

As we watched, aghast, more explosions lit up the skies with a cavalcade of fireworks. The sounds reached us some ten seconds later, less violent than the original.

'Oh, dear Modron!' Blodwyn gasped.

'What is it?' someone asked. 'What's there?'

Blodwyn's voice was subdued. 'An ammunition dump near Chorley.'

The lights flickered twice, before plunging us into total blackness save for the faint flickers of yellow shadows on our faces from the fire.

Whatever had happened there had affected us too. The whole building was as dark as a tomb.

2

Don't panic, everyone. The generator should kick in automatically,' Matron's commanding voice announced. We all waited, expectantly, afraid to move lest we fall over unseen obstacles. Nothing happened. Matron lifted a torch from her apron and murmured something in Welsh.

'Candles and matches, in that cupboard there.' She kept the feeble torchlight on whilst two girls lit a dozen candles and passed them around the ten of us; Cook, Matron and we antipodeans.

'Something must be wrong with the generator. It should have started immediately when the power went off. We have it rigged up in case there's a blackout when the doctors are operating. You, Sister Newton, and you, Nurse O'Reilly. Come with me. The rest of you, distribute more candles and torches throughout the wards. Cook will show you where they're stored.'

The light from outside was still visible with the popping of more explosions mixed with the faint sounds of fire brigade sirens. The whiff of cordite was there too, reminding me of happier days in Wagga on Empire Night when we exploded bangers and lit sky-rockets and Catherine wheels.

A soldier once gave me advice to try and associate that distinctive odour with Cracker Night, rather than gunfire and exploding shells. It had helped, especially when every one of my senses told me I was going to die.

Matron herded the two of us to what I assumed was the hospital's hub. Orderlies, other nursing staff and soldiers bustled around, seeming as useless as we were without proper light.

'Lieutenant Tamara. Thank goodness,' she said, reaching a man barking orders to others.

'Matron? And who are these women?'

He shone a torch in our faces.

'My new nurses. What can we do? The generator?' Matron and the tall, thin soldier reminded me a little of Laurel and Hardy with their contrasting shapes.

'Our generator is, pardon me ladies, well and truly stuffed. And the engineer is on compassionate leave. There's no one available to repair it. Worse still, there's some operation on a poor Spitfire pilot chappie who just crashed. They can't do anything in this gloom.'

'How large is the jenny,' I asked.

The soldier turned to me in anger. 'About ten-foot cube, you stupid woman.'

I glared at him. He actually called me stupid. 'I mean wattage . . . power,' I retorted.

He backed off, apologetically. 'No idea. Why?'

'I'm no engineer but my dad is back home.' My father ran a large company in Wagga with buses, earth-moving equipment hire and machinery repairs as well. Not having a son, I had been his apprentice whether I'd liked it or not. 'He taught me to strip down and repair generators. It's not one of those wood-gas ones, is it?'

Blank stares all around. I doubted it but they were popular now there were gasoline restrictions and were mainly used on cars and trucks.

'No, diesel,' a burly, young sergeant replied. 'I signed for the delivery last week.'

'Can you fix it, Nurse ... ?' the Lieutenant asked, feeling the pressure to make a decision.

'Sister Newton. What do you have to lose?'

He glanced at Matron who nodded.

'All right then, Sergeant. Take Sister Newton to the generator room along with whatever tools she needs. And you, over there. The exercise doctor. Go with her in case they need a hand with lifting.'

I hadn't noticed the thin, unassuming blond bloke in the background. He was in civvies, a doctor's whitish coat on top.

'My arm, Lieutenant. I can't lift.' He indicated his right arm hanging limply by his side.

'You're a lot more capable than our patients, Dr Carr. Do as I ask. Now!'

The man acquiesced, cowed by the tone of the chief officer of Killymoor Hall. Although he was a civilian, this was under military control. Even if it weren't, I doubted Doctor Carr would have stood up to the attitude of Lieutenant Tamara.

I gave a weak smile to Nancy as I accompanied the two blokes, our way lit by torch and candle. My clothing wasn't quite right for this yet it was preferable to my uniform. The Sergeant kept glancing back to check I was close behind. He wasn't that concerned about Doctor Carr whom I could hear, stumbling along behind us.

'Here, nurse. In the cellar. Watch out for rats.' The Sergeant held the heavy wooden door open for me. There were stone steps and thankfully a sturdy single-rail banister. The steps' edges were worn and shiny in the unnatural reflections from our lights in the oppressive gloom. The odours of mould and dampness mingled with the whiff of fuel. Scurrying sounds reminded me of the Sergeant's warning. Once the door was closed by Doctor Carr, we moved down the stairs.

'Head!' the Sergeant said, as he ducked his six-foot frame under a beam. Once at the bottom, he skirted around discarded furniture from bygone times, reaching another door to a more recently constructed brick room. There was no lock, only a heavy metal bolt which was open. I could see electrical wiring feeding through holes in the brickwork under the floors above.

I surveyed the beast that should have supplied power to the large Manor House. How they managed to install it was beyond me, unless they'd brought it in, bit by bit. It was relatively new. It would have to be if it cut in automatically in the event of a blackout or brownout.

'First things first, Sergeant. Check the fuel levels and that everything is switched on.' I indicated where to check the diesel whilst I verified all was superficially in order. The military wisely used diesel instead of petrol as it was less flammable. No point dismantling anything, if possible, even though the Sergeant had brought an assortment of tools.

Doctor Carr directed the light where I indicated.

'Can you run some fuel into a jam jar or something clear to see if it's contaminated with water or petrol, please Sergeant? You'll see separate layers if it is. Meanwhile, I'll check if the air intake has been blocked.' I was acutely aware of the time factor, especially for that desperate airman on the operating table.

The grease on my hands and clothing was a secondary consideration.

Doctor Carr called out, shifting around as though he were anxious. Was he claustrophobic?

'Come on. Let's get out of here. You can't fix it, Nurse.' That accent. I hadn't noticed it before. He was an Aussie.

'Not so fast, mate.' I could examine the intake while talking. I was intrigued as to why an Australian would be here.

'What's your story, Mr Aussie? First of all, what's your name ... your Christian name?'

The Sergeant was impatient. 'Concentrate on the job, please Sister.'

'I can do lots of things at the same time, Sergeant. All women can. Something to do with evolution.' I could feel something in the air-intake. 'There's something here, Sergeant. Cloth? Blocking the tube. I need a long wrench. Now, Doctor Carr. Your name and where you're from. And keep that darn torch steady.'

By this time, the Sergeant was by my side with the grasping tool. My fingers weren't that long.

I stretched as far as I could, turning my face to Doctor Carr. I was waiting.

'My name is Archie Carr. I'm from Sydney. Now, if you don't mind, I have to leave. It is too . . . I feel sick.' With that parting remark, he left, his hand over his mouth.

'Do you always have this effect on your fellow countrymen?' the Sergeant asked.

'Not usually,' I replied, very puzzled. It was almost as though he were afraid of me. I twisted my neck to stare at the muscular Brit. 'I almost have it. No wonder the jenny didn't work. No oxygen to help the fuel burn. It's really packed in tightly.' Finally, I felt the material budging and slowly dragged it free of the tube.

'There.' I threw it to the concrete floor, breathing heavily from the exertion. 'What is it?'

The soldier spread it out with his hands. 'A towel. You realise what this means, Nurse?'

I leant back, eyeing him. 'Yes. Sabotage. Coincided to happen with the explosion outside and the blackout. Best keep it to ourselves for the minute. And the Lieutenant, naturally. Now, let's start this beastie up. Fingers crossed.' Able to breathe again, the primed jenny sprang to life when we switched it on, flooding the cellar with a yellow flickering illumination.

I smiled at the Sergeant who nodded back. 'We make a good team, Sergeant. May I ask your name, or will you run a mile too?'

He laughed. 'You Australian women aren't backward at coming forward, are you? Don't you understand 'no fraternisation'?'

I wiped a greasy hand across my forehead. 'Considering fraternisation comes from the Latin word for 'brother', I don't see it applies to us in the literal sense of the word. I was simply asking your name. Nothing more.'

'Sergeant Tennyson, like with the

poet but I'm no Lord. First name's Ray. I'm from Manchester. Not that far away.'

'I'm Pauline Newton. From Wagga Wagga in New South Wales. Reckon I'll be seeing a lot of you, Sergeant. One thing I have to ask though. You appear to be fit and healthy. Why aren't you out there on the front?'

It was a perfectly natural question but the Sergeant's jovial expression vanished like a sheep at a dingo's birthday party.

'That's my business, Sister. We should report this sabotage immediately to Lieutenant Tamara.'

It looked as though my making new friends initiative was off to a very shaky start. However, I'd sorted out a major problem and discovered we had a fifth columnist in our ranks here. Quislings, like that Norwegian collaborator, were one thing but the thought that we had spies and even sympathisers in our midst was hard to swallow. Fighting the enemy was much harder when that enemy might be hiding under your nose.

Once back upstairs, we requested a private meeting with the Lieutenant. We went into his office where he first thanked us for our actions. The injured pilot was out of immediate danger.

The Sergeant opened the tool bag to show his superior what I'd retrieved from the inlet pipe. The Lieutenant's face was grim. What surprised me was the lack of proper military protocol between them. Rather than standing to attention to report our findings, Sergeant Tennyson was quite relaxed. It was a good thing we were in a room without windows except for an outside one, which was completely covered. Also, I was being included in this sensitive conversation and was privy to more facts than I felt was proper. It had been the Sergeant's suggestion that I stay.

'What was the damage, sir?'

The Lieutenant sighed; his anger barely restrained. 'The ammo dump.

Night-watchmen killed. We should be thankful for small mercies. The last shift had finished two hours earlier. An electrical substation and power lines, too. Well planned. As for our own espionage situation, we'll need to put a lock on that door. Next time it might not be as easy to fix.'

'Maybe a guard?' the Sergeant suggested.

'We don't have the man-power, Sergeant. We're a hospital. Or had you forgotten that?' At that point, I realised that a Lieutenant being in charge of a military hospital was unusual, certainly by all the protocols I was aware of. And, like the Sergeant, he was youngish and apparently fit apart from his amputated leg. The other soldiers that I'd seen all seemed old, disabled or injured in some way. Even Captain Franciscus at the induction had walked with a pronounced limp, using a cane to steady himself.

Well, if I was privy to this sensitive information, I might as well throw my two penneth in.

'Excuse me, gentlemen. It appears to me that the culprit who did this to coincide with the ammo-dump's annihilation must have had a reason for plunging this hospital into chaos . . . ?'

I left the statement hanging, hoping that someone might join the dots. If my suspicions were correct, then this wasn't an ordinary hospital stuck in the middle of Lancashire. Someone or something important was here and the German Abwehr had engineered a distraction for one reason only . . . to find them.

The two soldiers exchanged worried glances. The Sergeant began to open the door.

'Wait. One other thing. If you're going to check, don't go straight there. Do a full tour and include it in the middle. The saboteur might be watching you and waiting for you to reveal the hiding place.' All my father's detective pulp novels that I'd read as a teenager, had honed my own sneaky suspicious mind to a fine edge.

Agreeing tacitly, the Sergeant fairly dashed from the room, leaving me alone with a very desolate commanding officer. 'Lord, I hate this war,' he said, collapsing into his chair.

3

The Sergeant returned about fifteen minutes later, relief etched on his rugged features.

'It's safe,' he announced, breathing heavily. 'But one of the rooms has been ransacked.'

So, it was an object rather than a person.

'You're a clever woman, Nurse, sorry, Sister. Do you have any other talents we should know about?' the Lieutenant enquired.

I shrugged my shoulders, nonchalantly. 'A few.'

'Not just a pretty face,' the Sergeant said with a smile. 'Sir,' he added as an afterthought.

'Even with that grease on your forehead,' the Lieutenant mentioned prior to excusing himself to survey and rectify any damage. It was awkward being alone in the room for a moment until Sergeant Tennyson chose to speak.

'I believe you've worked out why two fit soldiers are here, Sister. Sorry I didn't tell you before. And please don't ask what is being guarded here.'

'I wouldn't dream of it. Loose lips and all that. Why confide in me though? I'm only a nurse. Not even British.'

'Better to have such a capable woman in the picture rather than snooping around on her own. You're curious, perhaps too curious and with a saboteur in our midst, we can't trust any of the resident staff here. Tonight, wasn't the first incidence of skulduggery. And let's not have you belittle your profession. I've been on the front line. Boulogne. Dunkirk. I've seen the bravery, dedication and skills of nurses. Besides, you might be useful as a spy for our side.'

I raised a quizzical eyebrow.

'Nothing dangerous. Simply set yourself apart from us. A few raised words about procedures, safety . . . that sort of thing. You versus the Lieutenant and me. If our German friend believes you aren't aligned with his enemies, you might learn more. We have to catch him and break this cell of fifth columnists. There are far too many targets for them around here . . . and a lot of civilian lives which could be in jeopardy.'

I hesitated for a moment. I'd always trusted my gut instinct to judge good people and Ray Tennyson was one of those.

'Very well, Sergeant. From now on I'll be a thorn in your side. We need to meet clandestinely though . . . to exchange information only, of course.'

'Of course.' He looked away from me then and there was a lengthy silence broken only by some shrill bird's song.

I was instantly enraptured. 'That bird? Is . . . is it a nightingale?'

Ray listened to the melody notes. 'Why yes, it is. They often sing, at night. Only the males though. Why ask?'

'Florence Nightingale? Nurses? But it's more than that. My grandmother used to describe their uplifting songs as one of the things she missed most about the old country. I can see why. It is so beautiful.'

We listened in silence some more, the war momentarily forgotten.

'You have birds in Australia?'

I laughed. 'Oh yes, wonderful coloured ones like rosellas and flocks of wild budgies. Mostly the ones around Wagga Wagga screech and squawk, grinding on your nerves. Cockatoos, galahs even kookaburras. Their laughing certainly isn't soothing. Bellbirds would be the Aussie equivalent but even then. To listen to your nightingale in the midst of this diabolical war . . . don't you feel it? It touches and restores a little of our souls.'

We made some vague plans after that, pausing every so often to revel in the melodic tones. Despite the assurances of my safety in this undercover role, I couldn't help but feel apprehensive. Being bombed or shot at by some unknown assailant was one thing; to be working with someone who secretly might want you dead was a new experience.

* * *

The Lieutenant arrived back and was appraised of our scheme. Again, the familiarity between the Sergeant and his superior was disquieting. If anyone were giving orders, it was Ray. Eventually, we moved to the door intending to put Operation Kookaburra into force. In the corridor, there were doctors and nurses bustling around on the late evening shift. Some wounded civilians had been brought in from houses damaged by the explosion. It seemed that, in these times of crises, the fact we were a military hospital, was a moot point.

'Thanks again, Sister, for your assistance with the generator.' The Lieutenant was getting the attention of those nearby.

I turned to him and the Sergeant.

'Least I could do, sir. Just make sure that mongrel Sergeant keeps his distance though. Just because I'm a woman, doesn't mean I'm on the bash.' I was as vindictive as I could be, pointing my finger at Ray who remained stoic in the face of my accusations.

'Whatever are you implying, Sister Newton? My men are beyond reproach.'

'Your bloody Sergeant tried to kiss me when we were fixing your jenny. Kiss me! If I hadn't whacked him with my wrench . . . ' The Sergeant said nothing but absent-mindedly touched his shoulder before glaring at me.

'Is this true, Sergeant?'

'No sir, absolute rubbish. Besides, take a gander at her. Face like a dog's behind. I've got better taste than to make a move on that, sir. She's dreaming . . . or desperate . . . or both.' I bristled with genuine anger. 'Face like a dog's behind' was really pushing this show past what I intended. I could have escalated the performance but I was supposed to be somewhat fragile.

The Lieutenant dismissed my accusations before suggesting I was forgetting my place and, if I weren't careful, he'd have me shipped back to Australia like my convict ancestors.

At that point, I burst into tears and left very hurriedly, my face covered by my hands. I reckoned if they awarded Oscars in England, we'd all win one. Sergeant Ray Tennyson would pay for that 'doggy' insult, though.

First thing in the morning I was up and dressed in full uniform, ready to join the others for brekkie before getting on with our first day.

Matron knocked and entered. 'We need to talk, Sister Newton.' I invited her to sit but she declined, our closeness of the previous evening seemingly a distant memory. That vindictiveness directed at Brenda yesterday was ready to be unleashed on me, my new role as Sister under threat. She told me what she'd heard and I gave her my account of his ungentlemanly actions.

It was only then she relaxed. 'It's not the first time my nurses have been in a compromising situation, Pauline. Sad to say, I believed Sergeant Tennyson was one of the ones with integrity. Goes to show. I thought three of you went downstairs into the cellar.'

'We did. There was that strange Aussie doctor, Carr, but he had a panic attack and vanished.'

'Ah yes, the Admiral,' Matron said. 'He's called the Admiral of the Swiss Navy by everyone. Thinks he's so important.'

I grinned. 'We'd call him Lord Muck. Wouldn't talk to me at all. Takes all sorts.'

Matron checked her fob watch. 'You eat your breakfast now. Take your time. I'll set the girls to work after I give them a talking to about the evils of men. My nurses always work in pairs. I want you to be Theatre Sister today. We have injured still arriving from Chorley. Your assistant?'

I considered my new charges. 'The

44

New Zealand lass, Ruth. Forget her surname. She's strong mentally at least. What about Brenda?'

'On sluice duty as I promised. We shall see if her attitudes change. I'm more a carrot rather than a stick manageress. I find it's the best way to deal with a stubborn donkey.'

I had a quick word with my nurses about their demeanour and decorum, impressing on them that a smile from a pretty nurse was often better medicine than any sulfa-powder for lifting the spirits. They were then paraded out by Matron whilst I tucked into my bowl of porridge. I was certain they would set a fine example, imagining them as they entered the makeshift wards before donning their aprons and getting to work.

When I joined them, it was clear to see they were all busy, even Nurse Isherwood scurrying to the sluice room. I was taken around by Matron, introduced to the doctors and orderlies as well as my British counterpart, Sister

Clara Denmead.

'Sister Denmead is from Leeds . . . in the county of Yorkshire, Sister Newton.'

Oh, strewth, I thought. Another dialect! For a country that invented the language, I reckoned they should all speak English the same.

'Sister Newton. Very pleased to meet you.'

What a pleasant surprise. I could actually understand her. Her speech was unlike other Yorkshirians I'd met. When I mentioned this, she explained she'd travelled extensively.

'You're from New Zealand, I hear?'

'Australia. About thirteen hundred miles away. Like here and Rome.'

'Goodness. That far. I'm sorry. My school didn't teach me much geography.' She gave me an apologetic smile, brushing a greying lock of hair from over one eye. I offered her a bobby pin but she declined. It was a polite, reserved greeting from the forty-something woman. She had a gaunt, surly expression that I always associated

46

with my female teachers.

Captain Franciscus entered the room, using his cane to limp along. His greying temples didn't detract from his rugged looks. He had a neatly trimmed moustache to complete the film-star appearance. There was blood on his gown.

'Ah, Sister Newton. Are you ready to scrub in? Some beastly injuries from that explosion, I'm afraid. A little girl will be our first case. Multiple breaks in her right arm. Some shrapnel, too.'

I took a deep breath, undoing my A.I.F. badge to remove my cape and beckoning Ruth over.

'Lead on, Captain.'

The next four hours felt as though we were on one of Henry Ford's conveyer belts. Captain Franciscus was focused, knowledgeable and supremely confident in his ability to do his best for his patients. The injuries to the child's limb were a challenge yet the doctor took it all in his stride, quickly assessing my limits.

Our next patient was from a nearby barracks, his leg immobilised in a Thomas splint with a five-inch thick cast of plaster of Paris. My team cut through the cast with shears prior to. him operating. It was an effective way of dealing with soldiers' limb injuries from the front.

At last, I was able to take a breather in order to assess how my nurses were managing.

It was an amusing interlude to discover a young nurse from Western Australia had been asked to shave the chest of a very hairy bloke. He'd taken one glance at her trembling hands grasping a cut-throat razor and sensibly suggested that he did the shaving while she watched and learnt.

Once we'd finished our shift and returned to our basic accommodation, there was a chance to sit with a brew in my own tiny room and take stock of the situation at Killymoor Hall. We had shortages of medical supplies but nowhere near as drastic as those I'd seen in Africa and Europe.

It was time for Germany Calling on the wireless. Though I detested the Nazi propaganda machine's attempts to encourage the allies to surrender by boasting of our losses to the 'superior' Nazi war machine, it was often the only source of up-to-date news. Britain's censorship was an iron-hand.

His awful voice began by taunting us with fabricated 'facts' about the Australians and others under siege in Tobruk, Libya. This was particularly close to my heart and it was hard not to accept Haw-Haw's put-on posh accent as being a pack of lies. He called them the Rats of Tobruk, a term meant to be derogatory and describing their penchant for 'borrowing' discarded German weapons and using tunnels to help baffle Rommel's forces.

I had it on good authority that our soldiers had adopted the name as a badge of pride. They were doing a fantastic job out there. Trouble was I couldn't share specifics, only point out the traitor's biased 'reporting'.

I could almost understand the Germans fighting for Hitler and his cronies. It was different for Haw-Haw. To turn your back on your own country and support their enemies was something altogether more abhorrent to me.

Haw-Haw then mentioned the destruction of the Chorley dump last night, 'right under the noses of the cowardly British military'. That incensed most of us clustered around the static sounds of the wireless broadcast, almost drowning out his pretend upper-class accent.

After he'd finished, there was a despondency in the air, finally broken by one of the British nurses announcing, 'Come on guys and girls. Let's have a sing-a-long before we eat.'

'There's a piano here?' I asked.

'A Joanna? Yes. Left behind by the owners. It's a bit out of the sun and moon, Sister, but I can still get a song or two out of her.'

I gathered this was a regular event. The ambulatory patients came to join in, even those from upstairs, some being assisted on their crutches. I noticed the Captain, Lieutenant and Sergeant lounging lazily against a wall at different times, enjoying the get-together yet not joining in. It was strange that the Captain outranked Lieutenant Tamara, yet it was the Lieutenant who was in overall charge.

After supper, I left the nurses to their free time. Matron wanted a word in the hastily fabricated office attached to the ward for our more serious cases. Sister Denmead was on duty with two nurses. We watched from the private room where there was a desk, two chairs and one of the drugs cupboards. The other cupboard was upstairs. There were two windows in the office to give a view of the now dimly lit ward.

'One of the roles of my Sisters is to dispense and monitor these drugs.' Matron unlocked the heavy metal cupboard door and gave me a list of the contents to peruse. Most of them were ones I was familiar with. Sulfanilamide and Sulfapyridine (or M&B 693) were the miracle antibiotics of the past five years. We used them to prevent bacterial infection in wounds and also for some of the nasty diseases which soldiers brought back home from sleeping with foreign women.

'Any problems with thefts?' I asked. The black market would pay well for most medical supplies.

'We used to have in the early days. Corruption, people looking the other way. That's why we have so few civilians working here now. Lieutenant Tamara arrived and cracked down. He brought in Sergeant Tennyson too.' She turned to me before locking the cupboard, checking it was secure and sitting down. She took off her shoes then sighed, commencing to give herself a gentle foot rub.

'A touch of gout; one of the joys of getting old although I'm told it's genetic.' Her dark stockings were laddered under her soles.

'By the way, Pauline. Keep an eye on

the girls and their stockings. Straight seams at all times.' I nodded. I thought I may have been guilty of that too. It was Matron's gentle way of giving me a nudge. I joined her on the other far-from-comfortable chair. She passed me the key fob with the keys she'd just used. 'Attach them to your belt. Trust me, you do not want to lose them. Your predecessor did. Now she's somewhere a lot less pleasant than this house.'

That explained a lot about my promotion. Blodwyn had done her research on me.

'Actually, I was quite taken aback by your accusation about Sergeant Tennyson's behaviour with you. I mean, you're a pretty woman and he's quite handsome. Not that I'm a betting woman or a budding Cupid, even though I would have thought . . . ' She left the sentence unfinished, a cheeky expression in her eyes.

'Ray? Yes. I must admit I was attracted. Not love at first sight, mind you . . . ' Then I realised I was talking out loud. Darn and double darn. I had to think fast. 'That was until he tried to kiss me. Without warning. I'm not that sort of woman, Blodwyn. I'm a country girl at heart; not 'Dirty Gertie of Bizerte' because I wear a uniform.' I assumed Matron knew the bawdy song. She did.

'I'll tell you one thing I've learnt over these past two years since Adolf invaded Poland. Life's too short, my love. Sometimes you need to take love where you'll find it. I lost my Elwyn in the first six weeks of this cursed war. Missing in action. All of those plans we had for a life together were shattered with one telegram. It had taken us so long to find one another. We kissed but nothing else even though he wanted us to. Now I regret my chasteness . . . every single day. At least we would have had those memories.'

I was surprised at Blodwyn's frankness with me. My mother would never have discussed such emotions with anyone, not even Mrs Ritzon, her bridesmaid and life-long best friend. Attitudes were changing. People were changing. Women were no longer 'the missus', raising the kiddies and looking after the home. All over Britain and Oz, they were doing the tasks of men, in the factories, on the land. It was a revolution born from necessity. I'd seen them working as air-raid wardens with their tin hats, ordering women and men to the shelters, driving buses and huge trucks. For all I knew they'd be out there, near us, manning ack-ack guns.

'Sergeant Tennyson's a good man, Pauline. Mark my words. You do realise what the British nurses call him . . . behind his back? Gary.'

'No. Not heard that.' Mind you, I'd only been here a day. 'Go on. Gary? No, wait. Gary Cooper.' One of my favourite movie cowboys. It suited him. And there was a resemblance.

Suddenly, I glimpsed two nurses rushing around in a blind panic. Without a second thought, I jumped up urging the Matron to do the same.

'Trouble!' We rushed out onto the ward. Both nurses were struggling to revive a patient, a young serviceman with an amputated foot. Sister Denmead was nowhere to be seen.

One of them saw us, relief flooding her features.

'Matron. He's struggling to breathe. It's getting worse.' We both gently pushed the girls aside, each examining him rapidly.

'Anaphylaxis. Tongue's swollen . . . his airway's closing up,' I announced, my mind racing.

'What has he been given?'

'Sulfa tablets. Stomach infection.' She checked his notes and her fob watch. 'Thirty-five minutes ago.'

'Where's the doctor?' Matron demanded. Both nurses looked around helplessly.

'We . . . we don't know,' one answered.

Matron cursed, this time in English.

'Fetch Doctor Franciscus from his bedroom. I don't care if he's fast asleep.

56

Bring him down here. Quickly.' The older nurse ran off immediately, her shoes clip-clopping on the tiles.

I stared at Matron. The patient had stopped breathing. By the time, Captain Franciscus arrived this young man would be dead.

And there was nothing we could do.

4

We've got to do something,' I said to Matron. Apart from the blocked airway, his blood pressure would have plummeted. 'Wait. Didn't I see Ana-Kits on the inventory?'

'Adrenalin? Yes. That would work. I'll get one.' We knew how long it would take. He still would be dead from lack of oxygen. Matron and I exchanged desperate glances.

'Do it!' she said. 'I know you can, Pauline.'

'Get me a sterile scalpel and scissors with six inches of sterile plastic tubing. And some black tape, Stat,' I said to the older nurse. Matron stared at me, momentarily before hastening to the locked cupboard. She realised what had to be done; a tracheostomy to allow air into his lungs.

I had performed this straightforward

procedure twice before under a doctor's supervision. This time I was on my own. I put a small pillow under his neck to extend his throat. The patient's skin was turning blue. Time was short.

Sliding my gloved finger down from his Adam's apple, I felt for the cricoid cartilage and commenced the incision in the soft spot in between. Then, having opened a hole into his windpipe, I inserted one end of the tube, blew through the tube twice then stood back, relieved to hear the sounds of air moving into his trachea and lungs. Colour soon returned to his cheeks.

Matron arrived with the kit about thirty seconds later and appraised his condition, nodding briefly before injecting adrenalin into him to help reduce the swelling. I put tape around the tube to help it remain in place. It was handy and really was used for anything these days from holding a nappy to repairing an aircraft wing.

The chlorpheniramine tablets that were in the Ana-Kit could wait to be administered. The priority had to be the adrenalin to reduce the swelling.

After what seemed forever, Captain Franciscus arrived, tattered dressing gown and one slipper on his feet, his cane by his side.

'What is going on here?' he demanded. 'Who did this?'

'I did, sir?' I admitted, unflinchingly. Hell. I'd saved this wretched man's life. He was conscious now but had been instructed not to speak or move too much.

Doctor examined the incision, peeling back the tape carefully before reapplying it. His expression was guarded. At last, he turned to me and said in a very gracious tone. 'What I'd like to find out is why you bothered to wake me up? The situation is well in hand, it would seem. Nevertheless, while I'm here I might as well pretend to be useful. Well done, Sister Newton.'

He then set to checking the soldier, explaining the situation. The sulfa tablets would have to be replaced by another therapy for his upset tummy.

Just then Sister Denmead appeared.

'Where have you been, Sister?' Matron inquired, her temper barely under control. 'We've had a near calamity here. Those nurses should not have been left alone.'

'Apologies, Matron. Call of nature. I was only gone a few minutes.'

'We'll discuss this at a more appropriate time. You should have ensured someone senior was here,' Matron replied.

'I did. Doctor Allen.' Sister Denmead scanned the room. 'Where is he?'

None of us had a clue. Matron nudged me. 'Come on Sister Newton. Time for a game of 'hide and go seek'.'

* * *

I was tired, my own adrenalin rush from that minor operation wearing off. Doctor Allen was apparently infamous for his 'pipe breaks'. Although cigarettes were allowed in wards the stench of pipes and cigars was too much for most sensible people in the confines of the supposedly health-restorative rooms of the hospital.

The normally competent doctor's preferred sanctuary was in the outside enclosed veranda. There was no lighting permitted out there yet he felt that gazing at the stars (but more often, British rain clouds) was the perfect place to light up his beloved briar and puff away whilst alone.

I had only met him the once, officious and not a lover of anyone in skirts. That included Scottish men apparently.

Matron explained all of this as we made our way along the rabbit warren of corridors of this, the original part of Killymoor Hall.

Few people were up at this time. Reading in the dim light of most dormitories was difficult, and, after an exhausting day, most staff were content to have an early night. There were a few men, listening to *When I'm Cleaning*

Windows, a jaunty little number from George Formby's film *Keep Your Seats Please.* I'd seen it a few years earlier in Wagga. Now I was living not far from his birthplace it seemed; a place called Wagon or something like that.

Nearby were some blokes playing dominoes.

'It's just through here, Sister. I'll give him 'what for'. Leaving those nurses to fend by themselves.'

We entered through a lovely stained-glass door into the narrow wooden-floored veranda that ran alongside the house. Ornate metalwork supported the roof panels and large panes of glass framed the once exquisite garden outside.

As it was a clear sky with a waxing moon, we could both see well enough without using our ubiquitous flash-lights.

'There's the little bathtub,' Blodwyn said as an aside before raising her voice. 'Oi, Doctor Allen. Since when are you paid to sit out here all night?'

He didn't respond. 'Possibly nodded off,' I suggested. The doctors, like us, worked long, exhausting hours. At last, we reached him, his silhouetted body seated on a cane chair.

Matron nudged him. His response was to slowly lean more to his right, tumbling off the chair with a thump. She immediately reached for her torch. The scarlet blackness covering him from his neck chest downwards could only mean one thing. Checking his pulse and touching his cold skin confirmed it.

The helpless doctor had been killed, murdered by a knife which was discarded by the skirting board.

* * *

'And no one saw anything?' Lieutenant Tamara was interrogating us at the scene of the murder, the once-clear windows to the garden now hastily curtained so that lights could be switched on to better examine the poor bloke's body. One thing seemed out of place to my eye, a dark blue stain on his hand, almost hidden by his frayed cuffs. The nicotine stains on his fingers made sense but not this.

Lord knows. I'd seen my share of dead soldiers and civilians but this one was so un-nerving, realising it must have been one of our own who did it. A few soldiers and medical staff were there, as was the Sergeant. He'd gently retrieved the knife but suspected what I'd already concluded — the perpetrator had worn gloves. There were enough surgical ones around.

'He didn't stand a chance, Lieutenant,' he concluded, eyeing me in a particularly disconcerting way. I tried to ignore him. 'I believe he must have been aware of the identity of his assailant, not suspecting their intentions until too late. Notice the expression? Total surprise. Also, the killer stuck his heart from underneath the rib cage — a professional execution.'

He stood back, regarding me. 'I hear

you're pretty handy with a scalpel, Sister Newton. Cutting someone's throat?'

Where the hell had this accusation come from? I was livid and just about to give this arrogant man a piece of my mind when Blodwyn placed a hand on my shoulder, gently restraining my forward motion.

'Sister Newton has been with me the entire time since before eight o'clock, Sergeant Tennyson. As others will testify, the good Doctor was alive and well at that time, attending to his duties. You are way off base, soldier ... that is unless you believe the Sister and I perpetrated this foul deed together?'

'As a matter of fa ... ' the Sergeant began, just as the Lieutenant interrupted.

'Of course, we're not accusing you of anything of the kind, Matron. Or you, Sister Newton. I'm of the opinion that whoever did this was an outsider who broke in. One of my men found a forced door. The Doctor must have simply been in the wrong place at the time.'

He touched his nose, avoiding my gaze. In my experience that was a sign that he was lying. But why would he be doing that? Then I understood. To admit there was a dangerous homicidal maniac in our midst would put everyone on edge, suspecting all of their co-workers and patients. It would also tell the villain, that we were on to him. He would then be on his guard.

This way, blaming an intruder, would deflect any concerns about there being a dingo in the chook house. I decided to muddy the waters a little bit more.

'I'd heard that there was a problem with gambling debts. Perhaps someone lost their patience?' I said this to the senior officer with a sneaky wink. Not that I was well acquainted with the deceased even though I was aware he had no relatives or friends to speak of. I hoped tarnishing his reputation a little would be tolerated if it were to help catch his killer.

The Lieutenant backed me up. 'Yes. I'd heard that, too. We'd better beef up security everywhere Sergeant. Can't have our staff being exposed to any Tom, Dick or Harry who decides that we're easy prey.'

'Yes, sir. I'll see to it immediately.' Whether Sergeant Tennyson believed the fabricated story or not was immaterial to me. I was well and truly cheesed off with his accusations and earlier insults. What had I ever seen in the man?

I stifled a yawn, seeing with more than a little satisfaction that the Sergeant had 'caught' it too. It was a reflex action.

'I'm off to bed, unless anyone still wants to lock me up for murder,' I said, pointedly glaring at my accuser. 'I have a long shift tomorrow.'

The Lieutenant waved me off dismissively. 'No, you go, Sister Newton. You too, Matron. Leave this terrible tragedy in our hands.'

Matron and I went back into the

inside of the Hall, each going our separate ways. I was half-way along a quiet hallway when I heard some noise behind me. I spun around, shocked to see Ray standing there. Unfortunately, there was no one else nearby in this part of the house.

'What was that about?' he demanded quietly.

'That was me being annoyed with you.'

He seemed shocked. 'But our pretend fighting between one another. Or had you forgotten?' he whispered loudly, moving closer.

'Pretend? Hah. 'Face like a dog's rear end' was a step too far, Sergeant. And just now . . . ? Accusing me of murder? Obviously, you have issues with me. From now on you do your job of soldiering and I'll stick to nursing. Our arrangement is over. Please excuse me now. Or do I need to scream?' The shock on his face was palpable.

Then I noticed something as he chose to leave, returning to where he'd come from. He'd walked by a relatively bright wall light on the ornately wallpapered wall above the rich wood panelling that covered the lower part of the corridor walls.

'Hold on. Is that blood on your shirt?'

He paused, locating a nearby mirror to check his shirt colour. 'I must have cut myself shaving.'

'At night? I thought men shaved in the morning?' I was now quite suspicious.

'Not all of us. Surely you can't think . . . ?'

I didn't answer. I was already walking quickly back to the murder scene, keeping my distance from the N.C.O. The Lieutenant was chatting with a Corporal but I chose to interrupt him.

'Lieutenant, would you please tell your subordinate to stop pestering me? Also, ask him why he has blood on his collar. Blood spatter from the murder, perhaps?' I was quite angry. Sergeant Tennyson arrived choosing to stand well away from me this time. Everyone's eyes could now see the blood droplets on his collar and shirt.

'Well, Sergeant?' The Lieutenant's voice was measured but clearly required an answer.

Sergeant Tennyson appeared taken aback. Gone was the quiet confidence and familiarity when the two of them were talking last night. He paused for a moment, thinking better than to take his anger out on me.

Eventually, he answered, 'As I told Nurse Newton, I cut myself shaving. See. There's some styptic powder on my nicks.' He craned his face forward to demonstrate the point to me and Lieutenant Tamara. There was indeed some white astringent powder of the often used aluminium sulfate that was applied to stop bleeds.

I wasn't finished. 'Styptic pencils are only supplied in officers grooming kits, Sergeant.'

His eyes darted all around. Even the senior officer was uncomfortable for some inexplicable reason. At last, the N.C.O. offered an explanation. 'I . . . I'm aware of that. I . . . I purchased my own. There's no law against that, is there?'

I'd made my point. 'Whatever you say, Sergeant. You remember what they say about people in glass houses? As for me? I'm off to bed . . . again. This time, Lieutenant, keep your bleeding lap dog on his leash.' With those parting words, I left, not looking back.

★ ★ ★

After another fitful night of sleep, I arose to my second full day as Sister Newton. I prayed it wouldn't be as dramatic as the previous one. The Reverend called on me to express his concern and offer support regarding the shock of finding the body. He was a kind man, dedicated to offering succour to those in need, especially with those soldiers suffering life-changing injuries.

I couldn't spend much time with

him, my duties being as pressing as they were. Naturally, there was an undercurrent of fear pervading the whole hospital. Lieutenant Tamara called around to assure us all that security had been augmented. Of Sergeant blinking Tennyson, there was thankfully no sign.

The main concern which was flagged up to me in the morning was dearest Nurse Brenda Isherwood. Surprising as it seemed, she'd managed to survive her nursing career so far, despite having an acute fear of seeing blood. I could not believe it. Neither could Matron.

'She'll have to go, Sister Newton. She's as much use as a lighthouse in a desert.'

I had to smile at that. 'Wait a minute, Matron. Didn't that exercise doctor ask for some help yesterday?'

'The Admiral? Yes. He did. Been asking for a while now. To set up equipment and generally keep encouraging them in their routine. He usually has a few in that gymnasium room at a time. Getting them mobile as soon as possible is a priority. Best of all, no blood to upset her. Two birds with one stone? I like your thinking, Sister. I'll arrange it right away.'

Brenda was one of my team. 'No, I'll do it. My responsibility.'

Me and my big mouth. I had stupidly thought that Brenda might have mellowed yet her bitterness towards me was as intense as ever.

'What do you want, Sister?' she sneered upon seeing me.

'Your respect, for one thing, Nurse Isherwood. There are other places you can be sent. A nurse with your problems regarding blood wouldn't be much use anywhere in this war. Perhaps you should be returned to Australia. They need factory workers there, I hear.'

That settled her down, if only for the moment.

'I have a proposition. There's an Aussie bloke who's doing work with the injured servicemen to restore their mobility, strengthen their muscles, helping amputees to walk again. He wants an assistant and I'm certain that the patients will respond well to a pretty face and a smile. What do you say?'

I could almost hear the cogs turning in that head of hers, under those golden locks.

To be truthful, she was an attractive woman, taking more care of her appearance than I did.

'An Aussie guy, you say? Is he decent looking?'

'Not for me to judge. You might not like him though. As far as I am aware, he's not married.' It was a not-so-subtle dig. Brenda smirked but didn't fly off the handle.

'Shall we go have a shufti at this quack then, Sister? Do you have any idea where he's from?' We were already heading to the room Doc Carr was using. I noticed a spring in Brenda's step.

'Sydney, I believe,' I replied.

'Another New South Welshman then. Oh well. There's one good thing though. At least he's not a cockie,' she said with a mischievous smile.

Arriving at the makeshift gymnasium, we could see there were four patients along with Archie Carr. It was clear he needed help as, whilst he was encouraging one bloke to strengthen his arm muscles to use a wheelchair, the others were doing very little. Depression from major injuries was the hardest thing many wounded service personnel had to cope with, at least in my opinion. Even those with relatively minor problems often came back so traumatised that they would be of little use to their families and their countries.

Surprisingly, Nurse Isherwood ignored the doc, immediately introducing herself to the other three. Their faces lit up immediately as she asked their names. It was an instant rapport as she encouraged them to show her what they could do.

A pretty girl and a challenge? They didn't stand a chance. Moreover, their conditions, bad as they were, didn't appear to be concerning her. She was one of those wonderful people who could see past the horrific damage to the person beneath.

'Hey. What are you doing?' Archie demanded irately. It was my turn to intercede.

'Doctor Carr. You requested some assistance with the patients. You now have a nurse, full time. Her name is Nurse Isherwood.'

The anger was still there with some other emotions. Suspicion? Fear? It didn't make sense.

'But she's Australian,' he persisted, clearly noticing her accent. Again, why was he behaving so negatively?

'So are you.' I pointed out the obvious. That caused him to rein back on his behaviour, his eyes darting between Brenda and me.

'And she's a Sheila.'

This was getting tedious. I decided to adopt a more belligerent tone. No more nice woman.

'Yes, she's a Sheila as you can plainly

see but I reckon a beautiful Sheila will be just the motivation your patients need to attend your sessions. You can see her effect on those three already. You show her what to do and she'll do it. As well as her personality and looks, she's competent and intelligent. Deal with it, Doctor Carr. She's the only assistant you will be given.'

His face went red as he struggled to keep his obvious male ego from aggravating the situation.

I was aware that our audience had grown, two other patients having decided to have a stickybeak. Everyone was enjoying the floor show.

Reason happily prevailed. 'Very well, Sister. She can stay. I must admit I'd forgotten how obstreperous you Australian women can be.'

'I'll take that as a compliment Mr Carr. Make certain you treat Nurse Isherwood right. Respect at all times. Otherwise, you'll have me to deal with — the 'Sheila from hell'.'

With that I turned to depart, feeling

the heat from his repressed anger on the nape of my neck.

As I left, it was with concern, wondering where my anger had come from. I was always confident but never a harridan like that. Something about the man brought out the worst in me. It wasn't even the derogatory term 'Sheila'. Heaven knew I'd heard that once or twice back home. Like wolf-whistles, it was an aspect of being a young woman we often had to contend with.

I was hardly through the door when I heard it open again behind me.

'Sister Newton?' It was Brenda. I stopped to face her. 'I just wanted to thank you. No one's ever said such nice things about me, not even my mum. And I wanted to apologise for being a bit of a dill with you. You know, on the bus. Anyway ta.' She smiled and returned to the gymnasium. Immediately I could hear her berating one of the patients for slacking off from his bench presses.

It was a good result.

That night, as I lay awake in bed, I listened out again for the sounds of the nightingale. There was nothing. I'd not heard it again after that first night with Ray . . . Sergeant Tennyson. That made me sad.

The bond we'd shared was as though the songbird had brought us together like a melodic Cupid. In my thoughts, the bird had left, realising that our disagreement had left it no choice than to fly off on tiny wings to search for two others whose love might endure longer than a few moments. Was it love, I thought, or was it some waking fantasy of mine, imagining that, in the midst of this bedlam, I'd found someone?

I dismissed Ray from my mind, trying to visualise our upcoming train trip on Thursday. A group of us nurses were having a girls' day out in some seaside place called Blackpool. I'd heard about Blackpool Rock some-where so it must have a rock nearby like

Ayers Rock or the Rock of Gibraltar. I'd read Graham Green's mystery book *Brighton Rock* when it came out just before the war but Brighton was too far to travel to.

Then I remembered. George Formby did a song about Blackpool Rock so it would be good to visit. The Rock of Gibraltar had been shrouded with fog when we passed by it so I'd never seen it.

There was a sound outside. Was it the nightingale? I went to my window so I could hear better. It wasn't bird-song. Just two voices under a tree not far from my room. One was a woman's. The other . . . I couldn't believe it . . . was Ray's?

Craning my neck, I pressed my ear to the opening. They were in the shadows, voices so subdued I couldn't make anything out. The only thing I was certain about was it wasn't English.

Ray Tennyson. What was he doing? I noticed the cloud moving from over the moon and pulled the curtain aside from the window in my darkened room to better see the mysterious woman to whom he was chatting.

As the moonlight lit up their faces, I could just make out her features; dark, long hair, pulled back and gathered in a ponytail, her clothing also sombre with a jumper barely concealing her curvaceous body. She appeared to be wearing trousers, a more practical choice for those in factories than skirts. To be wearing them outside was deplored by many, men especially. Whether it was from a challenge to their masculinity or because they hid the shape of a well-turned calf or bottom was immaterial.

Did I recognise her? No.

Was I jealous? No. Absolutely not.

Did I believe she and Ray Tennyson were up to something dodgy? Too bloody right I did.

The wind must have shifted direction because some object blew off my bedside cupboard onto the floor. The clatter startled me as I glanced to see what it was. Too slow, I realised they had probably heard it too.

I dropped the blackout curtain down again but it wasn't fast enough. They both saw my face before the moonlight vanished again. Whatever they were doing had been secret but now they were aware that I'd been spying on them.

One fact I was certain of. In war, any war, people were killed to keep secrets hidden.

And that didn't bode well for Mr and Mrs Newton's eldest daughter, Pauline.

5

My heart was racing. What would Sergeant Tennyson do? Break into my room to silence me. No, I decided. I was being over-dramatic. It was probably my paranoia seeping through from last night's murder. That cloak-and-dagger meeting outside my window might have been perfectly innocent. It probably was. Yet even when I dismissed his insult and suggestion that I might be the killer simply because I could use a scalpel, this rendezvous of his just now did not ring true.

There was also his attitude with Lieutenant Tamara as if he were the senior of the two of them. That simply made no sense at all.

I decided to have a gander outside to see if the Sergeant and the mystery woman were still there. They weren't. Clearly, I'd scared them off. My mind sifted through other possibilities. Maybe they'd simply left after concluding their conversation in some strange foreign lingo?

Arrgh! Why couldn't things be straightforward?

Sleep eventually came, as it always did, bringing back those nightmares of a strafing raid on our camp in Libya. I could still hear the cries of the wounded in my mind. Then there was the sight again of those who could no longer scream in pain. I curled up into the same embryonic ball I had then, whimpering softly to myself.

My little Westclox alarm awoke me. Time for another day. I took one look in the mirror by my bed and instantly regretted it; Not that I was a fan of make-up but some rouge and lippy would be a definite improvement on my greyish complexion. I needed some sun. Maybe I'd take a constitutional when the weather and time permitted. The grounds around the Hall were extensive and though the gardens had not been tended, replaced in part by vegetable beds, there were still nearby forests and even outbuildings like the Gamekeeper's Cottage. I'd make a note of the trails from that large painted map, framed and hanging in the entrance foyer which was obviously there to impress visitors.

The team and I were, fortunately, beginning to settle into a routine. The urgency of the numerous injuries from the explosion was now more manageable. New patients were coming in from the front-line while others were being discharged or sent for long term care.

Police had come to investigate the murder of Doc Allen but they'd deferred to a military investigation. I figured they had enough on their plates, being short-staffed and all. Then there was the matter of a countrywide black-market theft and sale of goods. The most concerning story I'd heard was the theft of diesel from depots and farms. It was seemingly big business.

It amazed me, that, in the middle of this conflict, there were always people who took advantage of the vulnerable, ready to break the law to make a quick quid or more.

On the plus side, Brenda seemed to have found her perfect talent. Patients took to her bright, bubbly enthusiasm like platypuses to water. Doc Carr grudgingly praised her when Matron inquired how she was fitting in. It was clear that he preferred not to talk to me. Did I have the plague or some other unmentionable disease? It certainly felt that way.

Normally us Aussies stuck on the other side of the world, loved meeting up with fellow countrymen or women. To hear someone speaking proper English always brought a smile to us expats.

I didn't have any contact with Sergeant Tennyson. If we noticed one another, either he or I would avoid passing by. That we weren't particularly fond of one another was, by now, common knowledge. Not that I cared.

Usually, he stayed away from the

wards and I avoided those areas frequented by military types. As to what he was doing about his so-called searches for Nazi agents, that was of no interest any longer. He could polish his little rifle or gun as much as he liked, as long as he kept his distance. I had better things to excite me. The nurses and I were really looking forward to our day trip to Blackpool.

On Thursday morning, there was much eagerness about our trip. It didn't matter that us Aussies and Kiwis didn't really have any clue about our destination, it was our first day away together. The other nurses were minding the fort, so to speak, whilst Matron accompanied us to the beach as a sort of chaperone-cum-guide.

It was an early departure on the bus to the station. There was no sign of the dawn though it was forecast to be a fine, sunny day. We were all decked out in our uniforms, Matron and I impressing on our charges to remember decorum at all times and to keep in groups of two or preferably three during our time there. The meeting arrangements for our return trip was made clear. We didn't want anyone to be stranded in some strange town overnight.

Matron had chosen Thursday rather than the weekend as we had more flexibility for a day off than all of the factory workers.

'Trust me, ladies. If we were to go on Friday night, for example, there'd be queues for miles at the train stations in Manchester. Even if the train did stop at Chorley, we'd never be able to get on. It would be far too crowded.'

As it was, there were no seats on our carriage and, in spite of the unspoken rule to stand for ladies, none of the men there seemed to have heard it. Well, I supposed it was an unspoken rule for a reason.

Consequently, it was a bumpy journey, being jostled around like leaves on a tree during a windy day. We nevertheless had a laugh between us, our anticipation of a great day out not being upset by anything.

The station at Blackpool was crowded with soldiers and airmen. I gathered there were some airports nearby. Matron whispered that they built the Wellington bombers here and that the Polish Air Force was based close by.

'Hey, why are all the directions and street signs blocked out?' Ruth asked.

It was Matron who explained that it was to confuse any Germans if they landed. We laughed at that. It was obvious where Blackpool's Tower was. We could all see it rising high above the hotels and houses, a mini Eiffel Tower here on the coast of the Irish Sea.

'Can't see any rock,' I commented to Matron when we reached the sea-side promenade. The plan was to catch a tram to the tower as a group then split up from there.

Matron stared at me as if I were the Wizard of Oz. So did all my compatri-ot's.

'Blackpool Rock?' I pointed to the

ocean and coastline in both directions. 'Where is it?'

Everyone burst out laughing. I couldn't understand the reason. Finally, Ruth took pity on me, indicating a lollipop a young boy was eating as he passed us with his parents. 'That, Sister, is Blackpool Rock. Be careful. It'll break your teeth if you're not careful.'

'Golly,' was all I could say. How embarrassing. Then Ruth explained the only reason they were aware of it was that another nurse who'd recently been there had shown them. I began to laugh too. It was going to be a fun day out.

Despite it being cool, with winter just around the corner, the sun was out and the skies a clear azure blue. Planes could be seen in the skies overhead. There was a nearby flying school to train new pilots. As we stood at the tram stop, I checked out the beach. It wasn't like Aussie beaches, the sand far from golden white. Donkeys were being used for joy rides for kiddies, with the occasional sandcastle being built enthusiastically by children largely oblivious to the war.

'Look at that bloke,' Brenda exclaimed. In the distance on the water's edge, a gent in a suit and hat had rolled up his strides, taken his shoes and socks off and was padding in the water. I half-expected a bunch of penguins to be joining him. The water must have been as cold as ice.

The tram driver was female; no surprise there then. All of us were craning our necks out the windows to stare at the imposing tower as we approached it.

We heard some soldier say to his friend, 'I heard Lord Haw-Haw boast that the Luftwaffe had destroyed the tower.' His friend had a clever answer. 'If they did, then our men must have had a busy night rebuilding it. It was there the next morning, just like nothing had happened.'

Matron chose to join in, such was the friendliness of this place. 'Haw-Haw also said Hitler doesn't want to bomb Blackpool because he wants it for his own personal funfair. You can't believe a word, that disgusting traitor ever says.'

'Hear, hear!' someone else shouted then the passengers broke out into a vociferous rendition of *Rule Britannia*. I found myself joining in.

We all had some hot broth and bread in a tearoom, not far from the imposing edifice. Some complimentary statements were made about us in our uniforms by the numerous servicemen on the street enjoying their own recreation. The work we did was appreciated by all the armed servicemen, soldiers, sailors and airmen.

There was an incongruity with the respect we were given and the totally different comments exchanged between the servicemen and 'ladies of the night'. I was glad Matron had insisted we wear our uniforms, especially for the younger nurses who might have been vulnerable.

I'd heard that Blackpool was rife with prostitutes and that, in true capitalist fashion, the town was a place where visitors were encouraged to spend their hard cash on all manner of diversions; the children their sweets and ice-creams, young adults dancing and entertainment and some of the older men, comfort wherever they could find it. As we emerged from the café, we heard a voice from someone seated on the footpath.

'Tell your fortune, girlies. Only a thruppenny bit. Learn about your future boyfriend.' An old woman with a scarf around her head was seated on an orange crate. On the pavement, there was a hand-painted sign saying, 'Madame Zelda, clairvoyant to the stars, sees all, knows all.'

'Shall I?' asked Lois. 'It's only three pence.'

'It's your money, Nurse,' Matron told her. Three pence wasn't much; a cake and a cuppa in the café. Lois moved to stand in front of the fortune-teller who now had a glass ball in her wizened hands. They were stained brown from tobacco, probably roll-your-own.

Madame Zelda smiled upwards as Lois handed over the coin from her tiny purse. The teeth that remained were the same colour as her hands.

'Go on, Madame Zelda. Tell me what you see in the crystal ball, please.'

The woman took Lois's hand in hers, examining the lines on her palm whilst consulting with some, to us, unseen visions in the clouded glass.

'Oh, I see love there, dearie; a tall, rugged soldier with shiny black hair and moustache. Oh, he is 'andsome . . . and kind. It'll be love at first sight. A lovely wedding in a church on a bright, sunny day. Yer mum and dad will be there.'

Lois pulled her hand away, suddenly upset.

'They're dead. Both of them. Consumption.'

'They'll be there, my lovie. In spirit. I can see 'em looking down on you from 'eaven.'

Lois relaxed, returning her palm. 'Will he be taller than, me?'

The mystic stared up at Lois's imposing stature. 'Oh yes. Well over six-foot 'igh, I would think.' Lois was entranced. She'd told me once she was afraid that she'd never find a man she could love who was taller than she.

Madame Zelda wasn't finished though. She went on to describe the marriage in detail; white flowing dress and veil, the priest presiding over them declaring their vows. I assumed that our clairvoyant had noted the crucifix denoting Lois's religion that she wore around her neck.

'And now . . . what can I see? Little ones. Three . . . ' A grimace from Lois. 'No, five bairns, three girls and two boys. Such lovely faces.'

Everyone was watching, transfixed by the 'performance'. When she'd finished with Lois, the others were like kiddies in a candy store, vying for who would be next.

That's why I was caught unawares when Nancy announced. 'Sister Newton.' Her voice was louder. Immediately the others changed to chant my name. Nancy stumped up a threepenny bit before I could object.

'Go on, Sister. It'll be fun,' Ruth said quietly, imploring me to agree. It was an awkward situation. To object would have spoilt their pleasure. Matron realised it too. 'What harm can it do, Sister?'

She was correct. Not that I believed in such rubbish but it might be amusing. Besides, it was a day to let my hair down, figuratively speaking. Heaven knew I hadn't had much time to relax and those sleepless nights weren't doing me or my normally strong constitution much good. I proffered my hand to the woman, reminding myself to give it a good scrub later.

'Let me see, my dear. What do we 'ave 'ere?' She examined my palm with a cursory glance before pulling it closer to her wrinkled eyes. Then she turned my hand over and back, tracing her broken nail along the line I believed was called the 'lifeline' by palmistry soothsayers.

A furtive glance to my eyes betrayed an expression of concern. Next, the glass ball. She returned it to its wooden cradle slowly sitting back on the crate, her back against the brick wall of the café. By now the bubbly interest and anticipation had been replaced by a solemn air.

'I'm so sorry, dearie, I can't do yer reading. The spirits ain't telling me nothing about yer future. It ... it 'appens. They just go quiet, that's all. I expect even the spirits get tired sometimes.' She handed the coin back to Nancy and let my hand go. In all this time while talking, she'd been staring at everything else apart from my face.

I heard murmurs of, 'Surely she must have seen something?' and, 'What does it mean?' The party atmosphere had vanished like a soap bubble in the wind. I had to do something.

'It's okay, everyone. I expect Madame Zelda was just overwhelmed by the number of suitors in my future. I plan on having a man in every port. Not one to settle down with a proper boyfriend for quite a while, I reckon. Still. All those kisses to look forward to.'

'Yes,' said Brenda, helping to bail me out. 'I believe Sister will even give me a run for my money, canoodling all those men in future. Just make sure you leave some for the rest of us!'

I gave her a grateful smile. She'd jumped to my defence when she had no need to. I'd realised that, despite the revelations of that first night at the Hall, Brenda had changed, making friends with most, if not all, of her country-women.

'Yes, Nurse Isherwood. I'll try not to smooch all the men in the world. I'm sure there will be enough for everyone here. Even you, Matron.'

The exuberance was back, albeit a little forced. It was made even more entertaining when an elderly uniformed officer plodded up. 'Hello, hello. What do we have here? 'Madame Zelda'? Come on, Gladys. On your way now. Can't have you cluttering up the footpath, can we? Move on, or you'll feel the bottom of my boot on your . . . you know what. Sorry ladies.'

Gladys grudgingly packed up and hobbled away, her back bent so that she had to stoop whilst walking. The Constable apologised if we had been troubled by her. 'Fortune tellers and their ilk; we don't tolerate them. Gladys used to be on the game, you know,'til her clients decided to go elsewhere. She still turns a trick when she can but look at her. Would you want to . . . ?'

Matron gave the officer a kick.

'Excuse me. Far too much information, officer, especially considering the nature of your audience.' The policeman hadn't noted the youth of some of our group, two of whom had their eyes so wide open you could see the whites all around.

'Good gracious. Many apologies, Matron. I had no intention of causing offence to your staff.' He expressed regret again before leaving us. Understaffed and pressed to keep the peace, it seemed macabre to persecute harmless psychics yet ignore the streetwalkers who plied their trade in plain sight during the day.

The group of us parted company then. We agreed to meet up later to watch the tower circus but, in the meantime, some of them wanted to take in a show on the north pier. There was some double act, Jewel and Warris, and a ventriloquist called Nicky who had a pet cat named Snuffles. The others chose to attend the dancing in the tower ballroom. Armed military were on patrol everywhere in case there was any trouble.

Matron and I opted for a promenade along the front. The weather was clement and the atmosphere convivial. It allowed the others to enjoy themselves, free of our oversight. In addition, Matron suggested that she wished to have a private word. There were items we needed to discuss.

'You look a bit peaked, Pauline. Not getting enough sleep?' Matron's voice was kind yet I felt as though I were being interrogated by some Gestapo major.

'It's nothing. Probably the change of climate. Killymoor Hall isn't quite the same as the Greek Islands.' it wasn't very convincing.

'You can always talk to me, you do realise?' She put a hand on my shoulder. Maybe she was right. I needed a confidant but my fellow nurses? It wouldn't have been appropriate.

'I . . . I had a letter from my mother a few weeks ago. It took five months to reach me. My . . . my dad is ill. He needs an operation. Probably already had it and I don't have an idea about what's happened. I keep writing but . . . well. It's not as though I can phone them these days and the mail is censored; 'redacted' they call it. I'm just so anxious. Me and my dad were so close back home . . . best of mates.'

'Whoever said, War is hell.' was exactly right. It takes away everything we loved and turns it upside-down. You shouldn't be here, Pauline. You should be back home in your wonderful country, just a phone call away from your family. No wonder you can't sleep.'

We strolled on silently for a few minutes, both watching two young girls flying their kites on the sands, oblivious to the realities of this dreadful conflict. To them, life was for playing and paddling and building castles with turrets where imaginary princesses lived safe and secure. I envied them their innocence, praying they could grow up without the pain of losing someone dear.

'It might be none of my business but there's a way I might help with the sleeping thing.' She gave me a weak smile. 'Phoning to the other side of the world is a bit beyond the capabilities of this aging Matron.' We both understood that even sending a telegram overseas was no longer the possibility that it had once been.

'Don't suggest brandy, please Blodwyn. Tried that. Just gave me a headache.'

'No. Something else. I used it when they told me my Elwyn was missing. It's an herb; called Valerian.' We looked up as two Spitfires screamed overhead on some training sortie, the noise just a part of life in this bustling, resort town.

'Any side-effects?' I asked. At this stage, I was prepared to try anything. Well . . . almost.

I preferred to put my faith in modern medication, not some concoction that witches would have once prescribed, yet I was prepared to try it. Blodwyn told me she grew some plants in her herb garden at the Hall. I agreed. After all, us Aussies were always prepared to give the unknown a go.

Just then, we saw a sight I could never, in my wildest dreams, have imagined. There, sitting on the sand on the beach below the promenade, was an elephant; a living, moving elephant. It let out a noisy trumpet causing everyone to stare.

'Must be from the circus.' Crowds were flocking to see her and the trainers. It looked like bath-time as the mammal squirted water from her trunk over herself and then over onlookers who had ventured too close.

'You'd never see that happening on Bondi beach,' my companion commented, grinning.

'Beg your pardon, Blodwyn. Which beach?'

'Bondi. In Sydney. Surely you've heard of it? It's where Doctor Carr came from.'

I racked my little brain. Blodwyn had pronounced it 'Bond-eh'. Then it clicked. 'Do you mean Bondi? I pronounced it as Bond-eye. I'd been there twice in the weeks I'd been stationed in Sydney. The sand had been so hot I'd had to run across to get to the waves.

'I guess,' Blodwyn agreed. 'You'd know how to pronounce it proper. A lot easier to say than some of our Welsh words though.'

'Wish I had my Box Brownie. They'd love to see a picture back home, especially Tilly, the baby in our family. She's only ten.'

As we drew closer, it was evident that it wasn't a random pachyderm visit to the beach. A sandwich board was set up next to Nellie showing the circus and showtimes. There was also a photographer.

Matron and I didn't need much persuasion to pose with the colossal mammal. We ordered three copies, one for me to send back home. They'd be posted to us at the Hall.

After that, we moved away from the hullabaloo to sit on a bench overlooking the beach and gently lapping waves. Though tempted to take my stockings as well as my shoes off to run my feet through the sands, I resisted the temptation. As Matron had said, we should not make a spectacle of ourselves. Bare calves might not be proper for a nurse in uniform, no matter where we were.

Instead, I let the coolness and soft texture filter through my stockings as I buried my wriggling toes in the sands. Blodwyn and I chatted about nothing and everything, with the ambience of seagulls squabbling and the smell of the sea relaxing us both. Sitting here, like this, was a little touch of paradise for me, the perfect tonic for the past days' drama and intrigue at Killymoor Hall.

I had my eyes closed, my arms stretched out across the back of the seat, my face tilted up to the clear skies, eyelids closed when Blodwyn chose to speak.

'I had a word with your Sergeant, Pauline . . . about you.'

My eyes shot open. Instantly I was roused from my reverie.

'You had no right,' I replied, guarding my anger as well as I could.

Her reply shocked me. Plainly, she didn't intimidate easily.

'I had every right, Nurse Newton. I'm responsible for the welfare and safety of my nurses and, like it or lump it, that includes you. I was concerned about you.'

I backed down immediately. She was correct. What's more, she was a friend. I would have done the same for any of my team if there were a personality clash with any of the other staff.

'My apologies, Blodwyn. Short temper syndrome.' Especially when it came to our favourite Sergeant, I was ashamed to say. 'Promise you won't put me on sluice room duty?'

We both grinned.

'Promise, Pauline.'

'What did my 'darling' Sergeant have to say? Nothing good, I assume.'

'Quite the opposite. He was full of your praises. He wanted me to apologise if he'd caused you any offence. He said he'd already tried himself but it didn't go well. Then he mentioned something extraordinary.' She paused as though she were trying to make sense of it herself. ' 'Remember the nightingale'. That was what he told me. Does that make any sense to you because, as sure as Winnie's cigar, it don't make any sense to me.'

My mind returned to that first night, he and I alone in the Lieutenant's office, listening to the sweet melody of our mutual friend in the trees. It was just before then that I'd agreed to be the thorn in his side, setting me up as a spy with my own agenda of subterfuge. How was Ray to have realised that the taunt about my face looking like a dog's rear end would have triggered such a feeling of hatred and betrayal? It was meant to be an act on both our parts, a performance for an audience that probably included our German agent. Sadly, I'd taken it to heart.

That bully at school, Jimmy O'Shea with his constant taunts about my resemblance to a dog, had undermined my confidence for years. He'd heard me when I'd been suffering from whooping cough and reckoned that I'd sounded like a dog woofing. The name 'dog face' had stuck.

'Yes. It means something to me,

Matron. Just don't tell anyone, okay?' We'd have to keep up our deception, Ray and me. But this time I'd accept him as being on our side. Whatever had I been thinking to believe he was a double-agent? There were still questions that required answers but they could wait.

'Thanks for telling me, Blodwyn. And I will try out that Valerian magic powder of yours. In the meantime, we should head off to the circus.'

Nellie the Elephant was already on the march from the beach across the tramway and road to the tower. It was time to join the others and enjoy the performance before an evening meal of fish and chips then heading 'home'.

★   ★   ★

It was dark when we all made our way back to the train station. The skies had luckily remained clear therefore there was some moonlight. It was the last train to Chorley for the night and was quite crowded. Even so, we'd all managed to grab a seat, being first in line. All the shutters on the carriages were closed, dull yellow light illuminating the space. We were tired and had thoroughly enjoyed our day at the seaside. It would be late when the bus picked us up at the station and very late when we returned to Killymoor Hall. But it had been worth it. I even had my own little piece of Blackpool Rock.

The sound of the clickety-clacks as the train steamed along was so relaxing. The occasional whiffs of smoke from the locomotive added to the serene feeling even if the incessant bumpety-bumps kept me from nodding-off completely.

That's why it took me a moment to realise we were slowing down although there was no station in sight when we peeked.

'What's going on?' Ruth asked as we rounded a bend. Clara opened the shutters a little more.

'There's some bloke waving a lantern

on the track up ahead. Must be a problem.'

We came to a stop and sat there waiting for what seemed like ages. Unusually, the engine was silenced too. That meant that it would be some time before it could build up steam to get going again. Even I realised that.

Then the solitude of the night was interrupted by a dozen popping sounds from up ahead followed by a lot more.

'Firecrackers?' Ruth suggested.

I recognised the sounds and, for the first time in weeks, felt really scared.

'Not crackers, Ruth. Those are gunshots.'

6

The girls immediately ducked down behind the seats. I looked around. None of the men in the carriage were in uniform so I doubted they were armed. All sorts of scenarios rushed through my mind. Was it an ambush? The gunshots were a distance away, maybe half a mile but, seeing as we were in a heavily wooded area, it could have been closer. Then the distinctive chatter of automatic fire. A Vickers machine gun. It sounded like that but what did I know? There were a few single shots followed by silence once more.

Whatever had happened was finished. At least I prayed it was so.

Almost immediately, the front door of the carriage opened and there were a number of apprehensive gasps before I recognised the engineer I'd seen at Blackpool. He was accompanied by a young corporal with a walkie-talkie in his hand.

'It's all right. He's the train driver,' I called out.

Heads popped up from behind the seat backs, the passengers breathing a collective sigh of relief.

'Could you please tell us what's occurring?' an older, officious guy inquired.

The engineer waved his arms indicating that we all sit down if we could. There weren't many standing in any case and they'd congregated at the rear of the carriage immediately the first shots had been fired.

'Calm down, please. It's an Army unit. They flagged me down. Some sort of kerfuffle up ahead. Some Boche. Our boys stopped them though. Just radioed through. Right corporal?'

'Yes, sir. The threat has been neutralised.' Both of them made their way through to the next carriage, presumably to reassure them, too.

There were so many unanswered

questions though. What was the threat and had we been in danger? Soon we could hear the engine getting up steam again. It was a waiting game. No way would we be on time to meet the bus.

Then the front door opened again and four British soldiers entered in full battle dress. The strange thing that I noticed immediately was that one of them wasn't wearing any insignias. This was unheard of in my experience. My toes curled. They were clearly some elite commando force. All wore helmets though, in the dim light, it was difficult to see faces. They turned to us then one left the carriage without reason.

'You right, Mr Wolf?' one of them called to him, obviously perplexed by his rapid departure. For a moment there I thought . . . no, it couldn't be. My Sergeant? Out here? Impossible. Nonplussed, the one who'd spoken, chose to address us, his companions standing at ease with their weapons.

'Ladies and gentlemen.' He ignored the three or four children there. 'There

115

was an attempt to derail this train by a cell of Nazi infiltrators. They had explosives on the track.' There were gasps from some of the ladies, holding open hands over their mouths. I heard a few sobs.

'You should be reassured that we have known of their plans for days and were able to intercept them before they could activate their nefarious plan. At no time were you in any danger.'

The same guy from the back spoke up. 'Soldier, did you capture all of them?'

I could see a sneer on the corporal's lips. The smeared camouflage paint didn't hide that. 'Capture? No sir. However, I can assure you they won't be attacking any more trains. They won't be doing anything. Full stop.'

The implication was clear. They were the enemy and this was war. Britain was fighting for its very freedom. 'This time it was Matron who spoke up. 'Corporal. As the train will be very late arriving in Chorley, we will all of us have missed our connections. My nurses and I require a bus to take us t . . . '

'Killymoor Hall. I recognise the Australian nurse uniforms. Rest assured, Matron. We shall radio ahead to make certain that none of you are inconvenienced any more than you have been. That applies to everyone else, too.'

It was very gracious of him and outside their remit of stopping sabotage, I thought. Already the engine was preparing to depart. What a way to end the day.

★   ★   ★

The station was in darkness when we did eventually arrive. We were almost two hours late. There were taxis and some trucks to help take the other passengers home. We were gratified to see a single-decker bus awaiting our group.

'Get a move on, you lot,' shouted the less-than-friendly young driver.

'Where's Arthur?' Matron inquired. I

reckoned that was the pleasant older bloke who'd first brought us to the Hall.

'In bed, which is where I should be instead of collecting a bunch of prissy women. I'm not getting any extra pay for working at night. T'aint right.'

By this time, we'd all scrambled on board and were seated ready to go. To our shock, the driver switched off the idling motor and opened his driver's door on the half-cab compartment.

'Where are you going, mate?' Nancy said. We were all totally exhausted and wanted to get to sleep at the Hall as quickly as we could.

'Off to ring my boss from that phone box. I want more money for this. Unsocial hours.'

I stood up opening the window more between the cab and the passenger interior. 'If you don't get this bus moving, sport, there's going to be a mess of strife . . . 'trouble' to you.'

He laughed in my face. 'What are you going to do, flower. Drive it yourself?' I was getting so tired of masculine arrogance.

As the interior lights were still on, I could see the driver's controls. Leyland Tiger, eight-point five-litre diesel engine; built early '30s.

'Yes, I can drive this. Double-clutching might be a problem unless I hitch my skirt up but this is just like the ones I drove in my dad's company. Pity you won't be there to see my legs though. You'll be standing out there, wondering how you'll explain the bus hijack to your boss. Don't 'spose you'll get any pay then, 'flower'.'

If looks could kill . . . Nonetheless, he sat down again, quickly driving off but saying nothing. Back in my seat, I sat back. Matron was on my left, Nancy and Ruth in the seat at the front of us. They gave me words of encouragement though it was Nancy who noticed me shaking like a leaf.

'It was a bluff,' she surmised, quietly. Keeping my voice low, I admitted I did drive my dad's buses but only around our parking depot.

'And there's no way I could double-clutch the gears for too long. My muscles aren't that strong.'

Matron added, 'Plus none of us have any idea where we're going. Not even me though I've done this trip dozens of times.' She shrugged her shoulders. 'Elwyn always said I had no sense of direction.'

Blodwyn was right. It would have been a disaster. We burst into giggles at the thought. The driver glared at me in his rear-vision mirror and I gave a polite smile back.

The next morning, I awoke, feeling a little woozy but well-rested. Blodwyn's plant powder had done the trick; a great night's sleep and no nightmares. Then I focused on my alarm clock. Eight-thirty? Oh, my goodness. I'd slept through the alarm.

Examining it, I could see it had been switched off. I recalled setting it then Matron lifting it up to check. The cheeky woman must have silenced it.

Breakfast was another surprise. Against the odds, Cook mysteriously found some honey from the bees that were in hives outside. I added it to my porridge.

Arriving on the wards much later than planned, it was clear that everything was running smoothly apart from one of the more able patients who was quite obstreperous with one of the nurses as she dispensed medication. In addition, my mind was thinking more clearly. Not, as it had been, reacting to the immediate situation. Somehow, I felt I could stand back and consider the whole picture for the first time since I'd arrived here.

Sadly, I'd been behaving like a competent nurse rather than a Sister. Okay, I'd been going through the motions without demonstrating the authority that a Sister should display. I owed it to myself and my team to step up to the role.

The rude patient had just made a particularly disgusting suggestion to one of the junior nurses. Matron, who was in another ward had obviously heard the comment and was ready to give the young man a piece of her mind. I waved her off to comfort the upset nurse.

Walking slowly to his bed, I examined his chart, aware that there was an attentive crowd of nurses who seemed to have nothing else to do. A few had seen me stand up to the bus driver last night and I imagined word had gotten around.

At that moment, I was quite happy to speak my mind to this obnoxious man but there were better ways than losing my temper.

'Excuse me, Private Reynolds. Are you feeling a little frisky?'

'Well yeah, I am. I been cooped up here too long. A man has needs, you know. In fact, I might even fancy you.'

I went to tuck his sheets in around him, giving him my best Cheshire Cat grin.

'You've forgotten something, soldier.

122

This is a hospital and not a place to indulge your immature fantasies. I'm sure that I can speak for all of the women here in reminding you that we are solely here to assist you to get better. Looking at your chart I wonder why you are taking up a valuable bed and our precious time. You're a malingerer, Private. And an unwelcome one at that.'

There were bursts of laughter from other men and the gathering of women. 'Furthermore, if you are as full of energy as you profess, I see no need to detain you here any longer.' I turned my head to one side. 'Nurse Freeman. Please contact this man's unit and arrange his discharge immediately please.'

The nurse acted straight away, leaving Private Reynolds wondering what had happened. My point had been made. Sister Newton would now be regarded as a woman who demanded standards and made sure she got them. As for reminding other patients to treat my nurses well, I didn't need to tell them. They'd got the message.

It was only later, over lunch as we sat together, that Nancy commented. 'Last night and now today, Pauline. I've seen a new side of you. What's more, people, especially men, underestimate you. At first, they see you as a woman who is traditionally weak and subservient then you show them what a strong person you are underneath. I just found out today that England only allowed women our age to vote thirteen years ago in 1928; only thirteen years ago. No wonder women still behave as though they're second-class citizens.'

I hadn't realised it was so recent. Britain was supposed to be the most admired democracy in the world.

'I think all of us Aussie women are different to those here,' I conceded. 'Because Oz was so hard to tame, we've generally been on a more level footing over there. There are a few right arrogant male Aussies who talk down to us but I reckon they're just thick-headed, their brains frazzled by the heat.'

Nancy agreed. What was the phrase? 'Male chauvinist' or something like that. In any case, we'd had the vote since 1902, just after all the states joined together to form our country. French women still couldn't vote apparently. One of the French nurses in North Africa told me that.

'Things are changing for women, especially here.' I had another mouthful of lamb's fry with some green beans and stale bread. The misshapen plate wobbled on the table. Seconds were all we could get these days.

The meal wasn't very appetising and I'd always disliked the taste of liver, even as a girl. I decided to change the subject as I forced myself to finish what was there. At least there was some tinned apple in jelly for dessert.

Nancy was in a talkative mood today. 'Wonder if the Yanks will join in the war? And if they do which side, they'll be on?'

Another nurse answered. 'Surely ours. The good guys, right? They were in the Great War. And they speak English . . . sort of.'

Yet another joined in. 'They have long memories, them Yanks. The War of Independence? Remember? It was the fact they won that Britain decided to colonise Australia. The Poms had nowhere to send their convicts to.'

Nancy piped up, excitedly, almost knocking her coffee over as she did so. 'Hey, yeah. Yanks beat the Poms in 1776 and Captain Cook discovers Oz in 1778. See, I do remember stuff from Miss Finn's history classes.'

They didn't exactly discover it. There were loads of Aborigines there already. And her dates weren't quite right either. England began sending convicts out to Botany Bay in 1788. There was no point correcting her, though. She had such a bubbly, happy disposition you couldn't help but like her and overlook any minor foibles she had.

'Anyway, Nancy. Almost time to go.

Drink up and I'll have to gulp this dessert down quick-smart. Otherwise, I'll have to chastise myself for being tardy.'

Just before we left the makeshift dining room, I saw Ray pass by in the corridor. He was in full dress uniform for some reason, medals on his chest and his hair parted and slicked down. He was impressive in a quiet, confident way.

I thought again about that secret meeting we'd discussed so that I could update him on what I'd discovered about our spies. The trouble was that I had nothing to report. Not a sausage. Oh sure, I'd discovered things about Ray Tennyson, if that were his real name. He had a secret life, an alter ego, just like that wireless and pulp novel character, The Shadow.

I wondered if, like The Shadow, Ray Tennyson 'knew what evil lurked in the hearts of men'?

Then I had a thought. Poor Doctor Allen. There must have been a reason for his murder. If only I could discover why, then we might all have a chance of catching this mysterious group of Axis agents. Ray had told me on that first night that he believed the head of the Nazi spy ring was in our hospital, disguised as someone completely unimportant. He was a methodical planner, calling himself 'The Mastermind' or 'Das Genie'.

Even though the train derailment had been thwarted and the would-be bombers dealt with, I had no doubt that they were not the team who destroyed the ammo-dump. I also feared they had much more devastating targets in mind as well as whatever the Sergeant and Lieutenant Tamara were guarding.

Gazing at the soldiers, staff, porters, nurse, doctors and patients wandering by, I couldn't help but wonder: who could 'Das Genie' really be?

7

Training and supervising the nurses was a full-time job in itself. Assisting with operations as well, pushed my endurance to its limits and, with the lack of sleep before last night, there were times I'd felt I couldn't cope. Now I could be myself again. I didn't care if Blodwyn's concoction was the sort of medicine given by witch-doctors. If last night's effects were anything to go by then I'd continue it.

After our evening meal, most of my fellow countrywomen went to the sing-a-long. I had other things to do. Another letter home for one thing.

Matron was busy elsewhere and I'd asked her if I could use her office. She had pens and ink on her desk and I had my own supply of scented writing paper which I kept with my personal clean undergarments.

I hadn't heard from my family in a while and wanted to give them this new hopefully permanent address. These days, 'permanent' meant more than a month. I realised that whatever I wrote would be censored for security reasons so there was no point in describing too many actual landmarks or situations.

Mum had always impressed on me, to adopt the correct posture when writing and I was proud of my penmanship. The fountain-pen my dad had bought me for my twenty-first coming-of-age party was at home in its case.

I missed the feel of it between my fingers. Ordinary nibbed pens were so much slimmer and the ones on Matron's tables had seen better days. Two had bent nibs.

Mum had told me that the written word was so much more important to get right so that I should always decide what I wanted to say, before putting pen to paper.

I chose my words in my thoughts,

mentally checking the correct spelling for each and discarding those words I was not sure about. Then, ready as I would ever be, I opened the bottle of black Quink on the desk and removed a sheet and envelope from my stationery box. I began to write, making sure to dip the nib in each time I sensed the ink drying out. Even so, there was an unavoidable small blob at the end of my return address at the top right-hand corner of my letter. Should I start again? I decided not to.

There was a ritual to writing, inquiring after the family and friends' health before commencing my questions about Dad then explaining why I was in England and how miserable the weather was here. My promotion to Sister was a step I was very proud to have achieved and I told them that. It was a fine line between boasting and humility.

What should I write next? About Blackpool? Maybe not. I took the pen end from my mouth, conscious of mum chastising me for doing that. Old habits. Instead, I put it on the blotting paper spread out on the top, a few drops of ink falling on the ball of my hand. Rats! The ink was hard to remove without scrubbing. I stared at it, my thoughts wandering. Who else had blue ink stains on their hands recently?

It was one of those mundane questions but I couldn't let it go. None of the girls . . . nor Matron. No. It was a man . . . one with yellowed finger-tips . . . The dead man, Dr Allen. My subconscious must have noticed it in spite of the shock of seeing the blood. He must have been writing and not had a chance to clean it off before relaxing out on the veranda.

What's more, had he been writing a message which our killer had seen? Perhaps that was the reason he'd been slaughtered?

It was a wild supposition but one worth investigating, even if it was only cursorily.

I hurriedly completed my own letter,

placing the signed sheet inside an envelope that I addressed. Finally, I blotted my return address.

If the dead Doctor had written anything, it wasn't in here so I asked myself where else in this vast mausoleum of a house might he have done his writing. I didn't know anyone that had the luxury of their own private writing area apart from Matron and the Lieutenant.

Generally, staff and patients who were mobile used the small alcove near the recreation area. I decided to start there. There was no point asking anyone if they'd seen him there just prior to him being killed as the murderer himself might overhear my enquiry.

Some surreptitious investigating, just like Nancy Drew would do, was on my agenda. There were a few men seated there playing snap. Sister Denmead was there, too, reading some whodunnit, her glasses perched on the tip of her nose. We exchanged greetings in a detached, proper way, before I approached the empty writing desk, brandishing my stationery box for all to see if anyone were watching.

I made a fuss of getting myself seated, rearranging the cushion on the wicker chair. All of the time, my eyes were searching for any little clue that Doctor Allen might have been there.

The rubbish bin was over half full and clearly hadn't been emptied for some time. It wasn't difficult to 'accidentally' drop my own reading glasses case into the bin, mutter, 'Oh, bother,' then rummage around for it. There were a cigar wrapper and band there. It would be easy enough to check with the Sergeant as to Doctor Allen's brand. I pocketed them as covertly as I could before resuming my writing preparations. This time my letter would be to my best friend from school who was now married with children.

Not that we were that close these past years but I needed to follow through on my pretence in case I was being watched. Spies watching spies. For me, it was a new way of thinking.

After writing a half-page, I stood up to stretch and survey the room. The desk was up against a wall with its cracked banker's lamp lighting the paper up. Sister Denmead was intent on her novel and four other blokes, had joined those already there playing their games. Two were doctors, enjoying their leisure break. A group of British nurses were chatting and I was interested to see Doctor Carr was there too, being unusually gregarious.

From the sound of it, the Admiral of the Swiss Navy seemed so apt as a nickname for him. What could I hear him boasting about? Meeting royalty? From the expression on the girls' faces, they were encouraging him to elucidate though not believing a word of his claims. In its own way, it was a game between them too. Anything to relieve the boredom.

Killymoor Hall had its own extensive gardens and forests with a river, the

Calder running along one boundary. It was too far for anyone here to walk to and from the village of Killymoor during the night with bicycling and horse-riding out of the question too. Only the military men overseeing the Hall had access to vehicles so, in a way, this was a prison for us all, even the doctors.

The village was described by one wit as a 'one-horse town' where the horse had died of boredom. There was a pub, The Queen's Arms, apparently so named after Queen Victoria had stayed there one evening when she and her entourage had become lost and sought shelter in a dreadful storm.

Poor Killymoor. Its only claim to fame was being found by a lost monarch.

There was a general store, bakery, butchers, blacksmith/garage and post office too according to Matron. Hardly a thriving centre of commerce.

It appeared that the nurses had tired of Archie Carr's tall tales and were now huddled together, ignoring him and intent on sharing confidences about their favourite subject, men.

Having lost his audience, he waved his hand to me and rose to head my way. Great. I didn't like the man, especially after my earlier less than amicable exchanges.

'Sister Newton. How lovely to see you,' he said, crossing the threadbare carpet runner then reaching me.

'Hello, Ad . . . ' I began before catching myself. 'Archie Carr.' I didn't like using his first name but to use 'Admiral' might have been a step too far. Unfortunately, I did have to work with him, or more correctly, Brenda did. If he'd heard my slip, he'd chosen to ignore it. Instead, he smoothed his slicked-back widow's peak and wiped his slightly greasy hand on a mono-grammed hankie from his trouser pocket.

'Writing home, I assume, Sister? Jolly good. Might I ask to whom?'

'Too right. It's to a school friend. Just

bemoaning the fact that we don't have any Vegemite over here. I really miss it. Do you?'

There was hesitation for a second. Vegemite was one of those tastes you hated or loved.

'I've been out of the old country for over ten years, Sister. Can't say it's a problem any longer. I guess if anything I miss the tucker more. May I see your letter?'

It was a strange request to make yet there was nothing that personal. 'Yes. I suppose.'

He went to the desk behind me, gliding rather than walking almost. Actually, the way he moved was quite distinctive. And gliding wasn't right, either. Slither? It was certainly a fluid movement.

Lifting the page, he perused it momentarily before replacing the paper carefully on the blotting paper, straightening it with both hands precisely.

'Exquisite handwriting, Sister. My compliments. Oh, my word. Pardon my

138

rudeness. I should have explained my reason for my curiosity. My hobby is graphology; the science of studying hand-writing. I wasn't prying on your content, merely the style of your writing, Sister.'

Well, that was a relief. His interest in my letter was obtrusive and normally regarded as quite improper, permission having been given or not. As for graphology, I was aware of the techniques and belief that our writing reveals the real us inside. It had more credence than fortune-telling. That much was certain.

'What, pray tell, does my scribble tell you then, Doctor?' I wondered. My foray into the future with Madame Zelda had been less than disappointing. Perhaps this journey to expose the inner me would be more rewarding.

'Oh, I'm no expert, Sister. If anything, a gifted amateur. Saying that, I count as my friends, many entertainers and landed gentry who have regarded my revelations as remarkably intuitive and accurate. In your case, I can see that you are close to both your parents and have strived to excel in whatever you do for them, more so than your kind self.'

So far, so good but I expected that, already having met me, he would be privy to a great deal of information that would allow him to make more suppositions than genuine hand-writing analysis. Nevertheless, it was a pleasant enough diversion, totally unexpected given his earlier indifference and even antipathy to me.

'You are driven, confident and precise, expecting others to attain the standards you set for yourself. The flourishes on your 'y's and 'g's tell me that. The precision comes from the perfect fifteen-degree angle and the one-centimetre . . . sorry, half-inch gap between words. The size of your letters tells me that you are confident though not flamboyant.'

He glanced down at my page then to the left on to the blotting paper.

Immediately, some subtle change occurred. He stepped back, massaging his injured shoulder.

'That will have to do for tonight, Sister. I normally charge for such an analysis. Regard yourself fortuitous to have been given it free.'

With those parting words, he turned on his heels and left me there, mouth open in shock. Talk about mercurial. The arrogant man has approached me, behaving in an almost civilised way before changing topsy-turvy like into the ultimate drongo of the week. Was it me? I didn't think so.

Moreover, I now had concerns for Brenda who worked with him. To be fair, she'd seemed happy enough so maybe there wasn't a problem between them. I would need to ask her, though.

Realising how upset I was, Polly, one of the Brit nurses, came over and gave me a restrained hug. 'Don't fret about him, Sister. He's often like that. No one likes His Nibs, at all. We used to think all Australians were like him until you and the others arrived. That's why we might have been a bit snooty with you lot to begin with. Now we know you're okay.'

I thanked her for her compassion, deciding that His Nibs was probably more derogatory than the Admiral. At that moment, I decided that a few other even ruder terms might be more appropriate.

Some doctors believed they should be sitting in God's chair up in heaven. Doctor Carr was something else, though; an enigma far out of place in this generally amicable community.

Most of the rest in the common room had left, presumably for ablutions or bed. Only three nurses were left. I checked my watch before returning to the letter, quickly completing it and addressing the envelope. It was only when I was packing up my glasses and papers into the box that the well-marked blotting paper caught my eye.

What if . . . and I did realise it was a longshot . . . what if, Doctor Allen's letter had been dried on the hodge-podge of black and blue ink-stained paper? I could see 'I love you' clearly in reverse print all by itself on a small white area. Was there a message from the dead Doctor here as well? I could recall in the aftermath of his death, the Lieutenant announced that there was nothing in Doctor Allen's pockets. If the victim had discovered something and written about it, the killer had possibly taken it, never realising the blotting paper also might disclose the dead Doctor's concerns.

I had to tell the Lieutenant. Leaving at the same time as the nurses, we switched off the lights one by one. It took a few moments to locate him. The Lieutenant was with some other soldiers who always appeared to be around. I wouldn't have thought so many military sorts needed to be here as it was just a hospital but I'd not considered it before. As always in a hospital, there were others milling around which was fine as I did need an audience.

'Lieutenant,' I said loudly. 'I wanted a word in private about that horrid Sergeant of yours. He's been making disgusting propositions to me yet again.'

Lieutenant Tamara was surprised. 'Oh, it's just you Sister. What has he allegedly done this time?'

'Allegedly? How dare you . . . you tin soldier, you.'

'Please calm down, Sister. I don't want you having a conniption fit. Come into my office where we can discuss this privately.'

I was ushered in, each of us playing our parts in the tiny performance. Only once we were inside, did I give the Lieutenant a smile. He made a show of telling me off loudly one more time before offering me a chair with a cushion on it and speaking more quietly, inquiring what I'd discovered or suspected.

I detailed my deductions, confirming with him that Doctor Allen did have ink stains on his hands though no letter or message had been discovered. Furthermore, he told me that the Doctor's tiny room had been disturbed by someone prior to the death being discovered as the Lieutenant had immediately sent a Private there to seal the room off. He'd been too late.

'Could you send someone to retrieve the used blotting paper on the desk but make it look like a general clean-up?' I requested. He wound the lever around the dial on the internal phone before speaking to whoever was at the other end. It wasn't a proper phone. He told me it was called an intercom, short for 'internal communication'. It was hard to keep up with all the new words.

We waited patiently, hardly talking, until a corporal knocked on the door, entered and passed a large rubbish bin to us. He'd used another door that wasn't onto the public areas.

'Bad news, sir. The only sheet on top was virgin. Beg pardon, ma'am. Totally unused.'

I swear I saw the twenty-year-old

blush. He was dismissed leaving the two of us alone again.

'I can guess where the sheet you saw is now, Sister. On some fire. Seems like some other person had the same idea as you.' The Lieutenant crashed his riding crop across his own desk in anger.

'Maybe he took the wrong one? Look in the rubbish bin. When I rummaged through there, I did notice another sheet of blotting paper, all screwed up. Worth a look.'

There was Buckley's chance of discovering anything meaningful but maybe we didn't need to. Obviously, the potential lead had been taken because it could have been incriminating as far as identifying Doctor Allen's killer. That meant one of the individuals in that room with me was responsible. The timing was too coincidental; to take the paper within minutes of me leaving was proof they'd been there.

I jotted a list of individuals and gave it to the commanding officer. Top of the list was Doctor Carr. The trouble was we had no proof nor any idea of his contacts or schemes. My only consolation was that we were getting closer to finding Das Genie.

For half an hour we pored over the unscrewed-up paper, trying to discern any word or words that might suggest what he'd written. That he'd used it was evident. His back-to-front name was the first . . . and only discovery.

'I'll send it off to the boffins. Perhaps they can separate the blotted words. Wouldn't count on finding anything of import though, Sister. It just looks like a mess of black and blue splodges to me.'

I yawned. Beddy-byes time.

Before I left, I had to ask about Ray Tennyson.

'Where's Sergeant Tennyson tonight? Catching up on his beauty sleep? Or is he out train-spotting like last night?'

Lieutenant Tamara didn't bat an eyelid. 'In bed, I imagine. A touch of an upset stomach.'

Considering the state of the meat

available, the explanation was quite feasible though, I suspected, hardly true.

The officer suggested an exit that wouldn't betray my late-night rendez-vous. I took my stationary box and bade him goodnight. At least tomorrow would be more mundane with no dramas to upset my delicate disposi-tion.

One would think by now I would have learnt there was no such thing as a quiet life in Killymoor Hall but, in my defence, I was dead tired.

* * *

It actually did begin as one of those days when everything was going well. The staff were motivated and able to spend some more time caring for the patients rather than being annoyed by any awkward ones who seemed to regard nurses as their own personal slaves. Even Lance-Corporal Windover was mobile, moving his body to search the meagre stocks of our hospital library for his choice of book rather than asking a nurse to find him one then complaining that it was one he'd already read. He had a broken humerus, not a broken leg.

'Why don't you stretch your legs, Sister? The weather is fine and I need someone competent to go to the Post Office in Killymoor to collect some medicines that should arrive today. The Postmistress will telephone to confirm they're there. It will be an opportunity for you to see more of the estate if you don't mind a bit of mud on your boots.'

'Are you certain, Matron?' I asked. We were in Ward D at the time so proper protocol was required.

'Absolutely. I'm certain that Nurse Collingwood would permit you to use her bicycle if you wish. You can ride a cycle, can't you?'

I could, but a walk through the leaf litter and autumnal forest on the path to the village was appealing. It was only a few miles either way. Besides, I could post those two letters. A pity there wasn't a faster way to find out how Dad was. We were so close and the thought that the 'strong man' who'd always been there in my life might be really ill was a major concern. I'd send that photo with Nellie the Elephant later.

It was a strange sort of communication these days. I tried to write once a week but, more often than not, life got in the way. If I replied to one today it might be to a letter which they'd sent months ago and we'd both written in between. That meant a very convoluted jumble at times with no sequence between what was sent and what was received.

I'd given up on writing to most of my pen-pals. The War made that too difficult, by half.

* ★ *

Having been told the medicines had arrived, I set off at the beginning of my lunch break, choosing to go in more sensible attire than my nurse's uniform. There was apparently some scrambling down banks and up the other side on the well-trodden and signed footpath through the undulating countryside. 'Little Ghost' brook might be flowing swiftly and the bridge was in some need to repair.

I'd studied the route map on the large painted plan of the estate and so was confident I wouldn't end up in Whitby by mistake. Not that I knew where Whitby was but it was a name that I'd heard a few times since being here.

It was brisk but enjoyable to be outside. The buildings of Killymoor Hall were soon lost from view leaving me uninterrupted vistas of trees, fields and dry-stone walls. Even a few birds came to join me on my 'adventure'. Then, to one side, I noticed a browny-red animal shadowing me in some long undergrowth and brambles.

It was a fox; my first live, honest-to-goodness fox. I'd read about them, of course. Two of them were in Rupert books, twins from memory. I'd also seen dingos in Toronga Park zoo. I 'spose they were the closest thing we had to foxes and wolves.

'Hello Mr Fox,' I called out, cheerily. He, if it were a he, didn't reply but I was undeterred. He continued to track me and I yakked to him until we finally parted ways as the path turned right towards one of the forests.

I shivered as the cool northerly wind picked up a bit, prior to tightening my scarf a little more. The prospect of traversing the forests with their deciduous trees was intriguing. There weren't any forests like this, certainly not near Wagga. There might be the odd garden with fruit trees or maples but proper Aussie forests of gums kept their leaves all through the year. Again, all those British books I read with exciting adventures in the woods gave me dreams of how it would be. To finally experience those dreams of fungi growing in the moist, aromatic smells of rotting vegetation evoked positive emotions in me. Once more I could push worried thoughts of Dad to the back of my mind.

As the trees grew thicker, the rotting leaves under my boots became squishier rather than crispy crackles. In a particularly dense part, I decided to pause, breathing in the aroma and magical aura as they twined around one another. The canopy above was gently raining down leaves of gold and red and tangerine, eddies catching the foliage and politely requesting a dance or two as they fell.

I brushed oak and hawthorn leaves from my shoulders and was about to move when I was grabbed and hurled to the soft bed of leaves upon the soil, brushing against ferns as I fell.

I was being held tightly by a man. As I gathered my breath to scream, a cold hand clamped me across the mouth and his face loomed over mine, scant inches away.

'Don't scream,' he whispered, his hot

breath nuzzling my ear. 'If you do, we're both dead.'

8

I was about to bite his hand when I stared at the man's eyes so close to me. His body was sprawled across mine, his other hand pressing against my waist to stop me wriggling free.

Those eyes were intense. The lower part of his face was covered by a balaclava.

'Stop struggling, Pauline. And listen.'

His rough wool mask grazed my face as I realised his hand was moving upwards over my stomach. Then he lifted it to his face, keeping my body immobile with his own. He tugged the wool up over his hair revealing his features to me.

'Ray?' I tried to say before seeing that anger in his eyes. The pressure of his body on mine was hurting so I tried to shift, pushing him away.

My goodness, I thought. But what

was he doing, forcing me down between clumps of undergrowth? Then I heard them, three voices coming our way.

'What you doing, Trigger?' It was a young woman's voice.

'Thought I heard some noise over here. We don't want anyone spying on us, do we?'

'Course not, you plank. That's why we do the exchange out here, in the middle of nowhere.'

Ray pressed his face to mine, our lips brushing against one another, both our breaths coming fast. I could smell his fear that we'd be discovered.

Trigger's voice was closer now, the sound of leaves rustling as he kicked them. 'I was sure there was a noise, right over that way.'

'You're paranoid, Trigger.' It was the second man, older with a strong Scottish rasp to his voice.

'Naw. I'm C of E, me. Can't see nothing around here.'

'Probably a squirrel, Trig.' It was the girl again. 'Come on, you two. Let's finish the transfer then you can have your money, Trigger.'

I realised now that Ray was doing his best to cover the colour of my clothing and white petticoat with his own camouflage clothing. Despite the danger, however, the pressure of his body on mine was making it hard to breathe. I felt a cough starting and struggled hard to suppress it, holding my hand over my mouth.

'What you going to do with your dosh, Trigger?' the girl asked. They were moving away now, back to where they'd come from. Thank goodness for that. Ray rolled off me, breathing a sigh of relief. I played dead though, trying to listen to what they were saying.

'Maybe a girlie or two. Don't suppose you'd be interested, my flower?'

She laughed. 'There ain't that much money in the world, Trigger. You really do stink, you know. If I were you, I'd buy myself a bath.'

We stayed lying on our backs staring up at the denuded canopy overhead, only relaxing when we heard two separate trucks start off and disappear down the lanes on the estate.

Ray stood up, brushing leaves from his fatigues and hair. Then he helped me up, giving me some belated privacy as I rearranged my garments and petticoat. There were no mud stains anywhere I could see.

I picked some icky millipede from my bodice, holding my top out to check for any other creepy-crawly stowaways.

'You didn't have to be so rough, Sergeant. Fairly knocked the wind out of me. Anyway, why aren't you armed? You could have arrested all three.'

He looked shocked.

'Sorry. That was uncalled for. I understand you were simply saving me from whoever those three degenerates were. Thank you.'

Ray cleared his throat, 'My pleasure, Sister. I wasn't carrying a weapon because this was solely reconnaissance . . . or should have been before you put your big feet in the middle of things. As for arresting them now? That would have forewarned the rest of their gangs. We intend to catch them all together. Regarding the identity of those people, it's complex. And the worst part is I didn't see the guy called Trigger. What are you doing out here, anyway?'

'On my way to Grandma's house, Mr Wolf,' I replied enigmatically using his code name from the train. He gave me one of his 'stop being nosey, Pauline' stares so I relented. 'Post Office, actually. Will you walk there with me in case I run into any more danger, please? Then you can tell me yours and I'll tell you mine. Deal?'

'I'm afraid not, Pauline. I have to trace that man, Trigger. Darn. I should have at least seen his face but I was too busy saving you from harm. Not that I regret that. It's . . . it's just, people put a lot of effort into learning where the fuel exchange was taking place. Sorry. I . . .'

I stopped him from going on anymore by stepping in front of him, standing on my tippy-toes and moving my mouth to his ear just as he'd done to mine.

'I think you will come with me, Ray Tennyson. In fact, I can positively guarantee it.' I moved away, touching his cheek gently. Then I began walking, twisting my head around to see him staring at me like a stunned mullet. As casually as possible, I dropped the bombshell that would ensure he'd be my bodyguard and confidant for the rest of the walk into Killymoor.

'I know who Trigger is.'

Ray was by my side in seconds. We were going to have a proper talk, whether he liked it or not.

★   ★   ★

Although continually pressed to disclose Trigger's real identity, I refused to do so until I had some answers myself. When negotiating, my dad had always told me to keep my trump card close to my chest.

'You're not a Sergeant, Ray Tenny-son. If that's your actual name. I doubt you're regular army either though you do outrank the Lieutenant.'

'It is my name. Not the sort of thing anyone would make up. But you're correct, Miss Smarty-Pants. I'm not a Sergeant. I'm with the Secret Intelligent Services, although I haven't been doing such a great job of the secret bit if it was that easy to see through my clever charade.'

I was sure no one else suspected and tried to tell him that. 'I'm quite intuitive, or so I've been told. Giving the Lieutenant orders in my presence didn't help. You seem quite relaxed together . . . almost like . . . '

'Step-brothers.' He shrugged his shoulders just before we both ducked down under a fallen bough. 'When Head Office realised there was an extensive network working out of the area, my brother was contacted and we spread a rumour that an important artefact was being hidden in Killymoor

Hall, the base for the Nazi Mastermind. There has been a great deal of subterfuge and damage done. What's more, he's getting more brazen, Pauline.'

'The ammo dump? The train?'

'Exactly. One of my Polish operatives gave us enough info so that we could stop the derailment.'

Polish? The girl outside my window that night talking to Ray. It made sense now.

'Your Das Genie. I reckon it's Archie Carr. He killed Doctor Allen, didn't he?'

Ray gave me a nod and a smile. 'My brother, Norman, told me of your suspicions this morning. It can't be The Admiral who killed Doctor Allen. The murderer was right-handed. Archie's right arm is so badly damaged, he can hardly lift it let alone hold a knife. And before you ask, no. He's not faking it. Captain Franciscus had to operate when it became infected and confirmed the tendon damage was there from a bullet wound.'

Rats. My prime suspect wasn't the murderer but I was sure he was involved somehow. I didn't trust the bloke at all.

Ray then explained what he was doing out in the woods earlier. Stolen diesel was big business on the black market and, although his team had pin-pointed the distributors, they'd wanted to identify the supplier then swoop on all of the criminals in one operation. Me stumbling in with my size six boots had interrupted that.

Finally, he had explained enough that I chose to put him out of his misery.

'Ray? You wanted to find out who Trigger is. I don't have his name but I can point him out. He's a driver in the Wright and Son bus company based in Chorley.'

'Brilliant. That's just what I need. How could you possibly have sussed that out, Pauline? Don't tell me you're a mind-reader like that Houdini guy?'

I laughed. 'Hardly. Trigger drove us home on Thursday night after the Blackpool trip. Arrogant little so-and-so. Likes to call women 'flower'. Thinks he's the Lord's gift. A bit like Archie Carr.'

I'd timed my revelation so that we were within sight of Killymoor. Ray went his own way to make some phone calls from the local police station whilst I ambled through the main street to the Post Office.

* * *

We'd arranged to meet back at the pavilion on the village green. Despite the rigours of war, it appeared that village cricket still continued although the majority of men of a certain age were still at war.

Certain professions were exempt from military service. Farmers, police, teachers and doctors were included so that meant a few of the regular players joined school boys and many older gents who'd thought their playing days were long over.

Ray was there when I returned, seated on a bench overlooking the pitch. The season had almost finished. I wondered if soccer teams of the same people would then be formed.

He offered me a sandwich which I gratefully accepted. My one from the Hall was a squished mess somewhere near where Ray had given me the shock of my life.

Whilst eating, I took my time to have a gander at the notice board. There was a hand-written poster telling us about the forthcoming dance at the village hall, something I made a mental note of. I loved dances. I was day-dreaming about them, my head in the clouds, when Ray brought me back to earth with a bump.

'I've talked to the police. There'll be raids simultaneously at five this evening. I'll need you there to confirm our target. Is that okay with you?'

'I shall have to check with Matron

but I don't see why not. I've been doing extra hours so a bit of time off should be fine.'

Ray brushed a crumb from my face and stared into my eyes so intently that I dropped my gaze to my lap, blushing a little. I was attracted to the man and I thought the affection was reciprocated.

'You're a remarkable woman, Pauline Newton,' said he, placing his strong hand on the back of my neck. I thought he might kiss me but the moment passed as he sat back, releasing his hold.

'But we shouldn't be doing this. Fraternising, I mean. We have to work together and the Hall is a tiny place when all's said and done. Besides you're not really my type. A bit too bossy and I do prefer blondes.'

Hold on. Where was this coming from? I couldn't believe what he was saying. Less than an hour ago, he'd been lying next me. Nothing had happened, well nothing too intimate.

I was angry. 'Sergeant. You seemed to

fancy me well enough earlier. You just called me 'remarkable', if my memory serves me correctly.'

'That was a mistake, Pauline. It was just an observation. I have a wife and I can't betray her.'

The revelations were simply becoming better and better.

'Next you'll be telling me that you have children . . . ?'

His face turned away and I thought I heard a stifled sob. Standing up, I turned on my heels, took the Post Office packet of medicines and marched off towards the forest and pathway home.

My life was complicated enough already. At least the situation with Ray Tennyson had been resolved before I'd made too big a fool of myself.

★   ★   ★

A uniformed Lance-Corporal collected me from Killymoor Hall under the watchful auspices of Lieutenant Tamara. I was driven to the bus depot where a plain-clothed police officer walked me around the expansive yard where buses of all shapes and sizes were garaged.

If anyone asked, we were on our way to the depot waiting room to catch a bus to Preston. It was my job to indicate the criminal called Trigger who was somehow capable of stealing quite a few hundred gallons of fuel over the past six months. At least, that's what the police suspected was the size of the theft.

It only took a few minutes until I spotted him, bold as brass, chit-chatting with two young conductresses.

Seated in the depot waiting room, my 'husband' made his excuses, saying he needed the loo before leaving and approaching Trigger under some pre-text. At his signal, four other police in uniform appeared along with the Lance-Corporal and Ray.

Spotting the police, Trigger tried to run but was brought down by an officer. Two other men also tried to escape but the net was tight and they had no chance. The other passengers and I watched through the dirty waiting room window as the drama unfolded before our eyes.

Having handcuffed the trio, Ray and two officers came up to the waiting room and entered. Ray gave me a cursory nod as a thank you, his features grim and determined for what he had to do next. This time he was in his Sergeant's uniform with the chevron of three khaki stripes, proudly displayed on his muscular shoulders.

From inside an office attached to the waiting room, an older, balding man came rushing out. He'd only just realised there was a major operation going on.

'What . . . what's the meaning of this Sergeant? Why are my son and two of my other employees in custody?'

His face was as red as a beetroot and he wasn't bothered about the spectacle he was making in public.

Ray didn't beat around the bush.

'Your son is a spiv, Mr Wright. Stealing diesel, probably from right under your nose.' The gathered passengers gasped. Although many people bought black-market goods, it was unpatriotic to be a perpetrator, especially for the fuel our boys needed at the front.

'No . . . that can't be. My boy is a good boy. He can't . . . ' The man burst into tears realising the truth. I assumed little things were now dropping into place in his mind; suspicions, conversations. Stealing on the scale that Ray had described would carry a jail sentence and fellow prisoners regarded diesel thieves in the same category as child killers. There was crime and there was patriotism. Even common villains had their standards.

The woman and Scots man would be in custody too along with others selling the stolen fuel.

After a few minutes, the Lance-Corporal entered asking me to accompany him back to Killymoor Hall. My role in the operation was finished and justice had been done. Why then did I feel so sad and depressed? One final wistful look back at Ray as we left answered that question. This bloody war made life's ups and downs so intense and rapid that it was really difficult to cope with the changes in emotions.

As the French apparently said in their own philosophical way, c'est la vie . . . that's life.

Us Aussies weren't so polite. My dad used to tell me 'Sometimes life sucks, Pauline'. I reckoned my dad's philosophy was heaps better. At this moment, I wished he were here to hold me closely like he always did when I was down.

I missed him.

★ ★ ★

Returning to the Hall, it was dark outside. For the first time since I'd arrived, I felt so alienated from it. The foreboding darkness from inside the shuttered windows didn't aid in lifting my spirits so it was with leaden footsteps that I climbed the entrance stairs to open the front door.

Immediately Matron saw me and came over. 'Thank goodness you've returned, Sister. I need some time to myself and require you to take over.' I only half-noticed the anxiety on her face but it didn't make any difference. There were enough of my own emotions to deal with.

'Where's Sister Denmead?'

'Visiting her auntie in Chorley. I did tell you.'

'Sorry, Matron. Other things on my mind.' Clara only had one living relative and she often cycled into Chorley to see her, not usually in the dark. Maybe a health concern. Her aunt had bouts of TB-related problems, according to Clara.

'Very well. Just give us a tick to get changed and I'll come down to relieve you on duty.'

Matron came up close to me to ask quietly, 'Are you all right, Pauline?'

'Yes,' I replied with a wan smile. 'Tickety-boo.'

⋆ ⋆ ⋆

To be honest, work was exactly what I needed. Otherwise, I'd be brooding and revisiting every minute event of the day in my thoughts. Even a momentary daydream of Ray lying close to me on the forest floor, whispering in my ear was enough to make me forget what I was saying to a patient.

Pushing that image to one side, I realised my cheeks were flushed and that both patient and Nurse Prendergast were staring at me.

As soon as I could, I dealt with evening rounds and retreated to Matron's office, collapsing onto her very uncomfortable chair. There I stayed, staring vacantly at the scene outside the window to the ward. My mind was elsewhere.

It was a rap on the window that roused me. I shook my head, focusing on the annoying noise. Brenda's face was staring back at me. She must have been there for some time.

'Sorry,' I explained. 'Away with the fairies. How can I help you, Nurse Isherwood?'

'Sister. I wanted to discuss one of the disabled patients if I may.'

I glanced at my watch. 'What? Now?' Then I saw her eyes indicating some urgency and that she was aware others were watching her.

'Oh. I see. Not Private Fellows again? You'd best come in again.' Two could play this game. I was aware that she had been treating the depressed young soldier and it was a good excuse to use his name. I was getting to be an old hand at making up stories to talk in confidence.

Once inside, I indicated the other chair, reaching for a pillow to make it a tad more comfy. These chairs were dreadful. 'I gather Private Fellows isn't the problem, Brenda? What's on your mind?' My voice was low and my eyes constantly searching outside for a sign anyone was spying on us. I hated being so suspicious.

'It's Doctor Carr . . . The Admiral.'

Instantly, she had my full attention. I leant across to listen more intently.

'Go on. He's not . . . you know . . . pestering you, is he?' She laughed. 'Him? No. I eat his sort for breakfast. I don't even think he's interested in me.'

'That's a puzzle in itself. In my experience men seem to prefer women like you. You are a bit of a flirt; no offence.' I was being honest with her.

'Maybe to start with Sister. But they're like boys with a new toy; at least the shallow ones. May I move on?'

I realised we'd been distracted. 'Please do. What's our Aussie doctor been up to?'

Brenda paused before staring outside to check there was no on eavesdropping. Goodness. We were getting as bad as one another.

'That's just it, Sister,' Brenda whispered. 'I honestly don't reckon he's Australian at all.'

9

I began to disagree. Archie Carr was as Australian as a jar of Vegemite. Then I paused. Archie had said something that at the time hadn't registered, as if he were bluffing his way through discussing it. Maybe Brenda had a point.

'You have my attention, Brenda. Please explain why you could possibly believe that?' Her eyes lit up. 'You suspect it too. Golly-gee. I thought it was just me.' Then she relaxed a bit and began to detail the reasons for her concerns.

'It's little things, Sister. He hardly talks to me and that suits me fine. I get on with my work with the patients and he does the more intensive stuff, setting up their regime with the weights and thingies. He's a bit creepy. Fastidious, too. Always polishing and cleaning furniture. Also, I've noticed he avoids all the Aussie nurses yet is quite happy to talk with the Poms . . . sorry, Brits. As I said, little things.'

Realising she was here this evening, I asked her what had happened today.

'Oh, today? He was explaining about good nutrition and stuff, talking about vitamins and minerals. Only he called them 'vitamins' — 'Vit' like rhymes with 'kit' and 'bit'. Like Brits say it.'

I smiled. It was a strange difference. Aussies pronounced the 'vit' as 'vite' like 'fight'. It made sense when you considered how we both said 'vitality'. We spoke the word properly and no self-respecting Aussie would screw that up.

There were other words too and places. In some ways, he appeared to have learnt to be an Aussie rather than really being one.

I related the reasons for my own worries; the Vegemite and mispronunciation of Bondi Beach to Matron. When Brenda asked me why some guy should masquerade as a person from another country, I suggested that there was only one reason that I could think of.

'Oh,' she said, realising the truth. Then she wondered about the next logical question. 'Why would a German spy be here?'

I explained that I had no idea.

But Brenda did. 'Maybe he's interrogating the patients here for information about troop movements and stuff?'

It was a strange thing to consider but Brenda must have had a motive for suggesting that. Her brow was furrowed as she tried to put the pieces of some intangible jig-saw together in her head.

I prompted her to explain.

'Well, not interrogate exactly. That's not the right word, Sister. Sometimes I get my words mixed up. It's just that Dr Carr has special sessions with some patients who come in for rehabilitation. He talks to them in a separate room, makes them relax and stuff. He explained it's to help them forget traumatic thingamebobs.'

My mind was racing. Separate room? Relaxation? 'Do you mean hypnosis, Brenda?'

'Oh, yes. That's what it's called. And he's always writing stuff in that little notebook he carries.' I sat there digesting all that had been said. It certainly appeared that Doctor Archie Carr was not the officious-but-harmless Aussie doctor that he purported to be. I'd have to let the Lieutenant in on this latest raft of information. From my viewpoint, Archie Carr might indeed be Das Genie, even if Sergeant 'married-man' Tennyson believed otherwise.

'I'm going to do some more investigation, Sister. Listening in, like.'

I didn't like the possibility of her being in danger, especially if Archie was Das Genie.

'Sister?' prompted the nurse.

'Brenda. Will you please stop calling me Sister when we're off duty like this? It makes me feel so old.'

'Righto. Cockie, then?' She gave me a impish smile which I returned in kind.

'What do you reckon, Pauline? Shall I be an undercover agent? I realise I'm not the brightest of women and that men only consider me good for one thing but I can do this, I really can. Imagine me, then. Brenda Isherwood. The nurse that stopped Hitler. Well sort of. My mum would be dead proud.'

I wondered if she were aware of the Shirley nickname, because of her long glistening curly hair. I made a decision. I'd ask her to wait before doing anything reckless, talk to the Lieutenant then work out a plan that would keep Brenda safe whilst still using her proximity to Archie to see what we could find out.

I told her in no uncertain terms that she shouldn't do a thing but continue with her normal, duties as though nothing had happened. Making her promise to wait made the most sense.

We parted as friends and I prepared to do my rounds of the wards. As I stood to adjust my cap and uniform, I noted an envelope in the otherwise empty bin. Being as curious as a cat, I retrieved and smoothed it out. It was empty but had been torn open. The word 'Matron' was neatly typed and underlined though there was no address or stamp. Someone must have delivered it personally.

Putting it back, I filed the discovery in the back of my mind. These days, I intended to make a note of everything, trivial or not. With saboteurs and a killer around, nothing could be overlooked.

★ ★ ★

The following morning, I searched for the Lieutenant. He wasn't there. Inquiries revealed he'd be away most of the day. Sergeant Tennyson was available but I chose not to talk to him, certainly not in private.

It was apparent that Matron had her own problems. She was vague and distracted, unlike her usual professional, focused self. When I inquired if there were anything I could do to help, she almost bit my head off, apologising later for being tetchy.

'Family matters. It's an issue I have to deal with myself, Pauline. If I do require advice, rest assured, you'll be the first one I ask.'

We left it with that but I decided to keep an eye on her, nevertheless. It was a good thing I did. When I noted her hands shaking as she was about to give a relatively straight-forward injection, I intervened without making a fuss. She left the ward immediately afterwards, his eyes misting with tears.

All the nurses had a buzz about them. The windy weather outside might have been the cause yet I suspected that it was the prospect for those off-duty tonight to attend the monthly dance at Killymoor Village Hall. For my antipodean colleagues, it would be their first, for others, it was a chance to doll themselves up, put on their prettiest frock and lippy and let their hair down for a few hours. The fact that there would be men there was a minor consideration as I suspected most would be too young or old to consider any hint of romance.

We'd be getting the bus there and back as the prospect of traipsing through the estate and woods at night was completely out of the question.

'You going tonight, Sister,' Ruth asked as we made a bed between us.

'Probably. Someone needs to keep an eye on you ladies, making sure none of the blokes there take advantage of you. I'm aware they'll be selling alcohol and the last thing I want is for some of my nurses to end up in the family way.'

Ruth laughed. 'No chance of that with me, Sister. I'm keeping myself pure for my Bobby back home in Christchurch. We're getting married when this war's finished.'

The exuberance of youth. To Ruth, the War was an interlude to her otherwise mundane, predictable life. She couldn't conceive that Britain, Australia and our allies wouldn't win and that the Nazis would be goose-stepping across England, and invariably the Empire as well.

There was talk of the Japanese becoming involved as well as part of the Axis of Evil. As for our 'cousins' across the pond, who knew where their allegiances lay?

Field-Marshall Rommel and his Afrika Corps were doing a lot of damage to our forces over there as were the constant threat of bombs here in Britain. No one wanted to mention the 'S' word but it was there as an option. Additionally there were still powerful people in Britain constantly calling for appeasement.

Yes, appeasement. That had worked so well the first time with Neville Chamberlain, yet they persisted. Sir Oswald Mosley and his now-banned British Union of Fascist Party for one. I mean, what could they be possibly thinking? 'Okay, Adolf. We give up. Just leave us alone to our fish and chips and games of cricket and we'll let you occupy the rest of the world. Pretty please?'

It made me so irate. And now there were Nazi spies in our midst, plotting Heaven knows what in the way of destruction and misery. At least there were people like Ray there to oppose them. We had our issues personally but that didn't mean I didn't like and respect him. He was a hero. He was my hero. It was a pity he was married.

Stop it, Pauline. You're daydreaming again. Besides. He said he only liked women like Brenda with her blonde hair and not being too bossy. Compared to her type, I wouldn't have Buckley's chance. As though she were reading my mind, Brenda arrived and headed straight for me.

There was a questioning look in her eyes that could only mean one thing.

'No,' I said firmly. 'I've not had a chance to check with the Lieutenant about that special device that you requested from Army Stores. When I do, I'll get back to you as soon as possible. That will be all, Nurse Isherwood.'

'But I'm sure he will approve. Can't I . . . ?'

'Please don't rush things, Nurse. These things take time and we don't want anyone injured by you rushing into trying this procedure by yourself. It wouldn't be safe.'

'If you say so, Sister. Just impress on him that I'm certain I can do it.' She scurried off leaving me wondering if I should ask Ray now. After all, he was technically the one in charge even though no one else was aware of it.

In the end, I decided not to. As it would transpire it was the wrong decision but it felt right at the time. That was the trouble with making choices. You must live with them for the rest of your life.

* * *

It was late when Lieutenant Tamara arrived back at the Hall. Very late. I was already dressed in my best (and only) party frock, ready to join my colleagues awaiting the bus.

I marched up, like Annie Oakley on a bad day. 'May I have a quick word, Lieutenant? In private. It's about Sergeant Tennyson . . . again.'

He glanced at his watch then back at my livid expression.

'Is this strictly necessary, Sister. Technically I'm off duty. I'm am entitled to some R and R, you realise?

'Oh, it's necessary. Wait until you hear what he tried to do this morning. Touched me on the . . . '

'My office. Now. Let's sort this wishful thinking of yours out once and for all.'

I slammed the door behind me and made a show of closing the blinds so that we weren't visible to the crowd of gossips outside.

Once we were hidden from prying eyes, Norman sat down wearily in his chair. I joined him on another on the opposite side of his neatly stacked desk.

'You look dreadful,' I said, compassionately. He seemed to have aged ten years.

'Bad news from the front. I wish I was out there doing my bit instead of nurse-maiding you lot. Sorry. That came out wrong.'

'I've seen your medical records, soldier. Your fighting days are over. You're lucky to be alive. I wanted to talk to you about Das Genie.'

His ears pricked up and he leant forward suddenly alert.

'Brenda Isherwood reckons that it's The Admiral. Says he's not Australian and I'd agree. Also, she has seen him hypnotising some of our injured patients.'

'Are you serious, Sister? Hypnotising? That explains a lot.'

He didn't elaborate and, quite frankly, I didn't have time for clarifications. I really wanted to go to the dance. I did discuss the possibility of her doing her own further investigations into our imposter. Like me, the Lieutenant was reluctant to sanction it, at least until we had someone there to keep an eye on her.

It was only as I was about to leave that Norman mentioned yesterday. 'Ray was very grateful for your input in the capture of that spiv and his fellow thieves. He thinks you're lovely, by the way. Intelligent, brave and a few other compliments.'

'Did he mention he saved me in the forest?'

Norman grinned. 'He did. We're very close but not as close as you two apparently were. I'm glad.'

'Glad? He told me was married with children. I'm surprised by your attitude, sir.'

Norman. removed his false left leg to rub the stump. He was in some pain yet here was I pestering him. 'You do realise they all died. Bombing raid on Leicester, eighteen months ago.'

That was a shock. 'I . . . I didn't. The way he talked, like they were alive.'

'Ray is a very private individual. In his mind, they're still here. It helps him cope. That . . . and his job which I gather you have been told about. Quite frankly you're the best thing that could have happened to him. His moodiness at times was causing him operational problems. Especially with this local Axis cell. Now, if you don't mind, I can hear the bus horn calling for all passengers. I believe you have a dance to attend, Pauline. Enjoy yourself.'

★ ★ ★

Most of the others were already seated on the bus when I arrived, giggling and laughing as young women do on such occasions. A few had rollers in their hair with a scarf tied on to help keep them in place. Some men were there too, staff, off-duty soldiers and those patients ready to be discharged.

I was about to embark wearing my only pair of stockings that were ladderless, when the driver noticed me and came over.

'You're that nurse, aren't you? I saw

you in the waiting room yesterday. You're the one what got my Louis banged up.'

Great. It was Trigger's father, the owner of Wright and Son Buses. Just what I needed. Aggro.

'Mr Wright,' I began but he cut me off, holding out his enormous hand.

'Wanted to shake your hand, missy. You did the right thing. My son's a spiv and a traitor, stealing money from the company. My missus, bless her heart, always told me he were a wrong 'un. Had two sets of books he did. Shoulda kept a watch on him but lately, since the missus died, it's all been a bit much for me. Now it's only me and my little girl left to run the company.'

He indicated the signage on the bus. 'Guess I'll have to get the sign-writer to remove 'and son', now. Won't be the same.' He dabbed a grease-covered rag to his eyes.

'You could always change the name to Wright and Daughter Buses?' I suggested. The old bloke rubbed his stubbly chin, musing on that for a moment, before flicking both his braces and breaking into a broad smile.

★ ★ ★

For a small town, there were certainly enough people there, eager to have some fun and frivolity. Children and elderly members of the community who could not possibly have danced had made themselves comfortable in chairs around the walls of the large but spartan building. The band, such as it was, tuned up on stage, the male singer and MC saying, 'Testing . . . One, two three,' over and over into the microphone on the chrome stand.

'Gee whiz. There's even bunting all around,' Nancy declared, her eyes alive with anticipation.

I'd noticed Ray and another armed guard in full uniform near the entrance, keeping a wary eye to make certain there was no trouble. There was a police wagon outside too, though there was no sign of a uniformed officer inside. He was probably off-duty, eager to jitter and let his hair down for a few hours.

When the festivities began, it was traditional dances that were first up; the Pride of Erin, Gypsy Tap and everyone's favourite, the progressive Barn Dance.

I was up there on the polished floor in my dancing pumps, smiling demurely at each new partner, be they a ten-year-old boy in shorts or an elderly man with wisps of greying hair on his pate and a wandering hand to test my patience.

Later, the more modern dances were announced though the older people persevered as best as they could before staggering over to the drinks bar, panting for breath after the unaccustomed exertion.

We twirled and whirled and kicked our legs high along with the off-key music from the band. One thing my mum had taught me to do when growing up was to dance. From being a lanky teenager to a confident young lady, I'd become proficient at the Black-Bottom, Boogie Woogie, the Gay Gordons and the Cakewalk.

I noticed my fellow Aussies enjoying themselves too, although Brenda appeared to have overdone it a bit. She headed towards the ladies on the far side of the hall, holding her hand over her mouth. Then someone took my hand and swung me around the floor. I found myself lost again in the frenzied celebration of release from thoughts of war, perspiration and excitement overtaking me.

When I next glanced over there, a man left the toilet area and walked quickly and calmly towards the door. He had a long coat on with collar turned up. That struck me as odd as it was a temperate evening, the heat from so many bodies mingling with the stoves providing warm snacks and soup for the attendees.

Then, moments, later another person emerged from the doorway. It was

Brenda. She was clutching her tummy. I excused myself from the dance and headed her way. Something she'd eaten?

I was halfway there when some woman screamed. I began to run. When I got there a group were standing around Brenda who was doubled up on the floor. It was then that I saw the blood; lots of it.

'We need clean towels. Now.' My voice was loud enough to be heard above the distressed wailing of some women. I was grateful that my nurses were there, used to dealing with a crisis and my requests. Rolling Brenda to one side, it was clear to me there was a wound on her right side. Blood was coming out and her own feeble attempts to stem the flow with her open hands simply weren't enough.

Kneeling by her side, I examined the injury. Brenda's eyes were closed tightly in pain. Immediately someone put material into my hands. I pressed it down onto the wound as gently and firmly as I could to stem the flow. Brenda moaned, clasping her hands over mine.

Ray dropped down by my side. 'What can I do, Pauline?'

'Get on that walkie-talkie or whatever to the Hall. She's been stabbed. We need to get her to Doctor Franciscus. You have a truck out there?'

'Yes. And there's a stretcher in the room here.' He waved his hands to two soldiers, one of whom was already on the radio.

Ray knelt down over my colleague. 'Brenda. It's Sergeant Tennyson. Ray. Who did this to you?' She was struggling to focus. Noticing the trail of blood leading from the toilets it was clear why. She'd lost a lot.

'Archie . . . Ar . . . chie Carr. Sorry sister. I . . . I was searching his . . . his book. Didn't think he saw me . . . Guess he did . . . '

'Don't talk, Brenda. And you Sergeant. Don't you dare think of chasing him. I need you with us.' I turned my head to the radio operator. 'Doctor Carr. Dark brown overcoat and trilby. Attempted murder.'

Ray and the others cleared the astounded onlookers to one side so that the simple two-pole stretcher could be opened at the side of my prostrate friend.

'I want a full search, Corporal. Bring him in . . . alive.' His orders were clear and concise. Nancy moved to the other side of Brenda joining me with the pressure compress. The towel was almost completely red but I felt that the flow had been stemmed. Nancy glanced at me, concern etching her own pretty face.

'Spleen?' she asked, staring at my blood-stained dress and arms.

I nodded. 'You'll be all right, Brenda. Sister's here. We're going to move you now. It will hurt. You ready?'

Brenda nodded, screwing her eyes even tighter in anticipation. Together, Nancy applying pressure on one side and me on the other, four strong men carefully lifted her onto the sky-blue stretcher then outside to the waiting truck.

Ray was on the radio all the time. The fumes from the exhaust of the truck were choking as we mounted the makeshift steps.

'Everyone ready,' Ray called from the front passenger seat through the pulled-back curtain to the cab.

'Yes. Fast as you can, but please no bumps,' I called out. Brenda was barely holding on and all the towels were blood red.

* * *

At the Hall, everyone was ready. She was rushed through to the operating theatre where others took over under the professional guidance of Captain Franciscus.

'Scrub in, Sister. We'll need you too.' I looked around. Neither Matron nor Sister Denmead were around. What's more, my arms and shoulders ached from the prolonged exertion of applying the pressure bandage.

'Right away, Doctor,' I replied. Changing as rapidly as I could, I could see my undergarments were ruined too. Time to worry about a new wardrobe later.

Sergeant Tennyson was there in the rear of the operating theatre. His ashen expression told me things were as bad as it could get. 'She's lost a great deal of blood, Sister. She'll need a transfusion or we'll lose her, almost certainly. Her blood type?'

'Australian nurses have discs around their necks.' He found it quickly, wiping it clean. In spite of his stoic English reserve, I could tell there was a problem.

'Type B rhesus negative.' I waited for him to continue. 'We don't have B negative or O negative in stock.'

If Brenda were given an incompatible blood type, she could have a haemolytic reaction with the immune system attacking the new blood cells.

'I'm B negative. You can use my blood, Doctor,' I said, producing my own blood type disc.

'Sister. A direct transfusion. I can't do that. The danger to you ... ' he protested.

'You can and you will, Doctor. Nurse, we need another bed in here. Stat.' I began to disrobe to expose my arm as Doctor Franciscus took up the challenge. He barked orders to the staff present and concentrated on repairing the knife wound and internal damage. Another competent doctor came to prepare me for the operation.

Soon I was lying down and connected up with tubes to Brenda. I could see how pallid her skin was. Both she and I would have had nine pints of blood but, judging from her appearance and what I'd seen, she'd lost almost two pints. A normal donation was just less than a pint. She needed more.

'Do your bit, Doctor,' I said watching my blood leaving my arm and trusting they knew what they were doing. I'd already told them to take more if needed. I couldn't lose Brenda.

Ray was there by the door, watching very anxiously. He was forbidden from coming any closer. I gathered that they hadn't caught Doctor Carr as yet.

My mind was becoming fuzzier and I felt myself drifting off to sleep. 'Doctor Franciscus. I think her blood pressure's falling too quickly.' It was Nancy's voice . . . I thought. I felt her shaking me.

'Pauline? Pauline? Wake u . . . '

10

When I awoke, the first thing I noticed was the pain. I tried to move but couldn't; I felt as weak as the proverbial kitten; one that had just finished a title fight with Jack Dempsey.

'Don't try to move, Pauline,' Ray said. 'We almost lost you . . . both of you. Don't worry. Nurse Isherwood is recovering in another room.'

I surveyed my room as best as I could. Clearly, there was only one bed — mine. The door to the outside was open. I thought for a minute I might be in a general ward with men but no. Someone was being extra kind to me.

'Some water, please,' I managed to say. My throat felt like the middle of the Nullarbor Desert.

Nancy popped her head in the door and, seeing I was awake, she came over to check on me. There was a saline drip in my arm, the skin of which was black and blue all over. It now seemed that my ruined clothing was the least of my worries.

All the time that she was prodding me, Ray was clutching my free hand in his. I hadn't noticed until he sweetly brushed an errant strand of hair back from my forehead.

'Careful, Sergeant. People might think we're friends,' I managed to mutter.

'I believe our subterfuge has no point any longer, Pauline. Our Axis infiltrator has been outed as Doctor Carr whom we still haven't apprehended. He's gone like a will-o'-the-wisp and taken that notebook with him. You were right and I didn't listen and . . . ' He stood up and hurriedly excused himself leaving me to wonder what was happening.

'Men don't like to be seen crying, Pauline. Surely you noticed his eyes. He's been with you all the time since you passed out.' I hadn't any idea he'd been there for long. Nancy wasn't finished. 'Did you realise you were anaemic? Cook said you need lots of liver.'

'I'd prefer to stay anaemic, thank her very much. I hate liver. Yuk!' I made a face and we giggled.

'What time is it?' I wondered. I could barely see daylight outside on the other side of the corridor.

'Fivish. You've been asleep all day. You must be hungry. I'll see what I can rustle up.'

With that she scampered off, leaving me staring at the ornate plasterwork on the ceiling. Talk about boring. White paint with some spider sitting lazily in her web staring back at me. How long would it be until I was on my feet again? Too long, I realised. If I were this cheesed-off after fifteen minutes, I'd surely go mad after a day and realistically I knew it would be at least that long before I could stand, let alone walk or get back to my job. I felt so guilty. Not only were we down a slimy, traitorous doctor (who actually was good at his job) but Brenda and me too.

Matron appeared in the doorway and could easily see I was awake. Yet she hesitated then turned and left, clearly realising there was something more urgent than talking with yours truly. I wondered whether I was suddenly contagious. Though if I were, it was only to her. Did she blame me for being the same supposed nationality as that fifth-columnist Archie 'the traitor' Carr?

I lay there, feeling sorry for myself, and irritated that no one was there to talk to. I had a million and two questions to ask but my hazy thoughts wouldn't let me concentrate. Instead, I began to count the number of petals on the ceiling rose simply for something to do. One . . . two . . . I was up to eighty-seven when Matron appeared again, this time deigning to enter the darkening room.

'Would you like me to switch on the light, Sister?' she asked formally.

I did and asked her to please do so. Standing by the side of the bed, she was every inch the imposing woman that patients, nurses and even doctors trembled in fear before. Her arms were clasped under her full bosom.

'How are you, Sister?'

'I could say 'absolutely rather spiffing' but that would be a fib and Father Black would hardly approve. Shall I simply say I've seen better days and leave it at that, Matron?'

It was best to return her unexpected reserved attitude in kind. Matron wasn't herself at all. Was it that letter she'd received or another worry entirely? Maybe she disapproved of one of her nurses being stabbed and then her Sister risking her own life to save Brenda? Who knew?

'Where were you last night anyway? We could have done with your assistance.' I asked irreverently.

'I was busy, Sister. I don't have to account for my actions or presence to anyone, least of all you. Suffice it to say, I had some news about Elwyn, my husband. He's alive.'

I sat up as best I could. 'Golly. That's great to hear.'

'You'd think so. It's more complicated than that,' she confessed, sadly. It was then I noted the haggard expression on her round face.

'I must be off now. This place won't run itself, will it?' She sighed, taking a moment to compose herself and walked wearily to the door. Before she left, she gazed at me and forced a smile.

'It's good to see you're recovering, Pauline. What you did last evening . . . I'm not sure I could be so brave to put my own life on the line for someone else.'

Then she went out, leaving me to ponder what was troubling my friend.

* * *

My solitary confinement continued, punctuated by bouts of activity in between long spells of exhausted sleep. I was fed and cleaned by my nursing colleagues. It was pleasing there was no liver; iron tablets being dispensed and swallowed instead.

Captain Franciscus popped in to sit and ask about my life in Australia before I nodded off once again. It was kind of him to do so. My initial impression of him being an old fuddy-duddy had proved to be quite unjust of me. Regarding Brenda, he explained it had been close. Her spleen and liver had been damaged but repaired. That a colleague of his, a fellow doctor, had done this to a young woman was totally abhorrent to him and obviously quite upsetting. He still refused to believe that Doctor Carr had murdered Doctor Allen. 'With that mangled arm of his, it would have been impossible, Sister. But in these days of unheard-of inhumanity to one's fellow human, who am I to judge what's impossible any longer?'

Ray returned the following morning. He looked as bad as I still felt. From his dishevelled appearance and thick dark stubble, I'd guessed he'd been up all night.

He closed the door.

'Don't worry, Pauline. Romance is the furthest thing from my mind even though you are lying in bed, ravishing as ever. I would have preferred you wearing a better nightgown than that but, truth be told, I'm simply pleased to see you alive and with some colour in those lovely cheeks of yours. And is that lipstick? How . . . '

'There are some very enterprising minds among our nurses here. And a few budding cosmetic chemists.'

'You are stunning. Victory Red is all the rage I hear. I gather that Adolf frowns upon Aryan women wearing any cosmetics or perfume. At least our Tommies have beautiful women to come home to. Probably explains why so many Nazis give up; nothing for them at home except women who look like men.'

We both laughed at that.

'Seriously, Pauline. I'm sorry for

telling you I was married. I do realise my wife and the boys are dead. I saw their bodies.' He wiped his eyes with the back of a grimy hand. My step-brother told me he'd explained this to you and I should have corrected you myself. It . . . it's just that to me, they're alive in my heart. I . . . I felt myself falling in love with you and it was like a tank that I couldn't stop. Everything about you is so perfect . . . well, except for that accent of yours. Even that I'm starting to embrace.'

I smiled and touched his cheek with my fingers. He leant his head onto them closing his dark eyes to revel in the sensation before gently pulling his face away and taking my hand between his to kiss it and run his lips over it in the most sensuous way imaginable.

'When you told me I was perfect, did that include my body?' I wondered quietly.

His face flushed red. I cast my eyes down to my chest and his eyes followed. Damn this bloody sexless gown I was wearing. There wasn't any décolletage visible at all and now my party dress was in ruins.

I heard whistling; Ray was intent on studying his fingernails, his cheeks flushed with heat again. Despite being married, I wondered if he'd ever seen his wife without clothing. We were between generations with some people still stuck in the Victorian dark ages.

Although I was a virgin, I knew what I wanted in my marriage and making love under the flannelette sheets in a darkened room wasn't what I planned once every week. Real love was more than that. A great deal more.

If Ray were to be the one for me, I'd have to take it slowly. Judging from the hurt he was feeling for his dead family, I could understand that.

The last thing I wanted was to cheapen his memories of what he'd had and lost. Now that he realised that we both shared an affection for each other, he'd come to me in his own time and on his own terms.

'May I kiss you, Pauline?'

'Do you have to ask?' I closed my eyes and felt a frisson of sensation as our lips touched then parted as rapidly as a nightingale flying by. It wasn't enough for me but it was for Ray. And, right here, at this instant, that was all I could expect.

He sat back as I opened my eyes and gazed languidly at him.

'Should you bring me up to date on the hunt for the villainous Archie. I gather you've been out there searching for the little toad.'

Ray relished the prospect of the diversion.

'Still no trace of that little Nazi weasel. He's gone to ground somewhere nearby, I suspect. Talking with his patients, it's become evident he was gaining information from them through some form of mesmerism. He'd been especially interested in the national artefact we have hidden in the Hail for safe-keeping.'

Goodness. I'd forgotten about that

. . . almost. The ransacked room on that first night when the generator had been scuppered; presumably by The Admiral or Das Genie.

National artefact? What could it be? Brazenly, I asked him.

'If the Axis cell hereabouts is aware of it, then telling you doesn't really matter, does it?'

I felt guilty. 'You realise I suspected you of being a foreign spy, Ray. At one time at least.'

He grinned. 'Can't blame you for that, my angel. My behaviour was very odd, especially with a woman as astute as you keeping an eye on me. That's the worst thing about this spying lark. When you can see the enemy in his uniform and metal stahlhelm, it's obvious who he is. Suspecting a colleague of being the enemy puts much more pressure on me and anyone I guess.'

Not wishing to make it evident that I spoke fluent German, I asked what a 'stahlhelm' was although I was aware it was a helmet. Ray apologised and told me.

'If you spoke German, Pauline, people might suspect you of being a spy. In my case, I speak passable German and Polish and a little French. Intensive training for my job. Most English-speaking people have trouble enough with English,' he laughed.

Ray then took a pencil and wrote two words on a sheet of paper, showed me, indicating not to say it, then took a packet of Red-Heads from his breast pocket and set it alight on a metal tray by my bedside. I'd heard about listening devices being planted in rooms though I doubted there was one here. Ray was being extra-cautious.

Crikey. Talk about the last thing I expected. 'If the Axis agents steal that and smuggle it back to Berlin, Hitler and Haw-Haw would have a field day propaganda wise.'

The Magna Carta? Here, secreted in Killymoor Hall?

Double crikey.

'It's not just that. We believe The Mastermind has a big operation planned for Blackpool. I can't say any more than that at present. Even though we've captured a number of infiltrators landing on the coast from submarines, some have made it through. Then there are the Brits who help them. They're the worst sort of traitor. Now, if you'll excuse me, Pauline. I must get cleaned up and grab some shut-eye. My informants have given me details of an operation due to take place later that we need to scupper.'

He was a bit whiffy so when he asked for another kiss 'for good luck', I held my breath. The things we did for love.

*   *   *

Once I was mobile and able to walk, I tried to visit Brenda but it was too far too soon to be on my feeties. Nancy plopped me in a wheelchair and pushed me through the midst of all the men who kindly asked after my state of health and when would I be back bossing them around. It was a morale boost and good to see people in a group again. The room could be so lonely and there were so many times you could count roses on the ceiling before you went mad.

I'd had a letter from my mum. It wasn't good news. Though the letter with redirection addresses hadn't taken as long as the last one, it was evident that dad's health was deteriorating. Mum had said he was due an operation but there was no way I could obtain more up to date information. It was so frustrating.

'Brought you a visitor, Brenda,' Nancy called out as we entered Brenda's room, if I thought I felt bad then it was a pale comparison to Brenda's languid demeanour. Seeing me, she brightened up, forcing herself to sit up despite the twinges of pain becoming more pronounced when she moved.

'My saviour,' she exclaimed, greeting me warmly.

Parked next to her in my chair, I took her hands in mine.

'Glad to see you made it, Brenda.'

She became quite contrite and reflective. I imagined that her life had flashed before her blue eyes as she felt the knife go in. 'I should have listened to you, Pauline. I took a chance and he caught me. He must have. I thought he didn't suspect but when I saw him holding that knife at the dance, I reckoned my time was up. I owe you my life.'

'Let's not be hasty, Brenda. Have you considered that you now have cockie blood in your body? You are well and truly contaminated now. How can you face your high-society friends again?'

'They weren't really friends, not like you and the girls here. Now, make yourself comfy and tell me all the gossip starting with you and the dishy Sergeant.'

The hours went much faster together, and it was exactly the tonic I needed. In turn, I helped her with her hair. I left after we shared our supper, Nancy wheeled me back to my own bedroom rather than the hospital one.

'Those rooms are only for sick people, Pauline. You're convalescing, so there's no reason you can't do it in your own bed. The girls and I bought you a coming-home pressie. It's on your eiderdown.'

'A pressie? Crickey. I'll have to get sick more often,' I said before breaking out into a coughing fit. I'd pushed myself too far today.

The gift, wrapped in a brown paper bag, was a new frock. It was stunning. And there were two pairs of stockings too, wrapped up separately.

'They're from the Sergeant. Friends in high places,' she joked, then helped me get ready for bed. I was asleep within seconds.

* * *

Each day saw me becoming a little stronger. I began helping out with paperwork for a few hours each day, building up my stamina to standing and assisting with light duties. Sister Denmead tended to ignore me whenever we espied one another. I assumed she was aggrieved at her extra workload although there was nothing which I could do about that.

Matron was still preoccupied and I often found her in the strangest of places, making vague excuses about doing inventories if I inquired. She and I had most assuredly grown apart. That was why it was perplexing that she should invite me on a walk around the Hall grounds the following day.

I was almost totally fit again, as was Brenda. She'd taken to supervising the rehabilitation classes from the comfort of her wheelchair in the so-called gymnasium. She was a natural at motivating the amputees and others to have a more positive outlook on their lives and futures.

'I thought we might wander over to the Gamekeeper's Cottage,' said Matron. 'The walk will be stimulating with all that fresh air and, even if not used now, the cottage has a lovely atmosphere.'

I'd agreed, hoping that she might take the opportunity to open up to me about the worries which were on her mind.

In bed, the night before our proposed woodland ramble, I turned off the light and lay back against the freshly starched sheets. I'd not heard the nightingale since that first night and was praying I'd hear it again. The autumn nights were drawing in and Jack Frost often kissed the windows as he passed by during the darkness.

I was reading a tattered copy of Thorne Smith's *Topper Takes a Trip* about Cosmo Topper in the south of France. It was funny and quite risqué, not the calibre of book a respectable young lady would read. That suited me fine.' Dad had always wanted a daughter who could set the points on a spark-plug rather than one who could embroider doilies.

I wondered if Brenda would like to read it once I'd finished with it. A noise from outside made me wonder if Mr Nightingale was back. His trills and melodic warbling told me he was.

Might I see him in the old cherry tree outside? I doubted it, though perhaps . . . I carefully pulled aside the blind only to be confronted by a man, about to knock on my window. Goodness. Realising it was Ray and not some total stranger, I opened the window to be greeted with a blast of frigid air.

'Let us in, Pauline. We need to talk. It's freezing out here.' Although speaking quietly, his voice was so loud. The last thing I wanted was him being heard. Coming into my bedroom was going to be poorly perceived if we were caught.

Nonplussed, I turned on the light and stood there, arms folded. 'Sergeant Tennyson,' I whispered back. 'I'm not that sort of woman. There are more appropriate times and places.'

'Please,' he begged, shivering under the crisp full moon. 'It's about Das Genie.'

Relenting, I opened the window, allowing the wind to blow in. The nightingale fell silent as Ray struggled to crawl through the space and drop down inside. He knocked my book onto the floor in his clumsy attempts to enter.

'Shusshhh!' I told him, panicking.

I closed the sash pane as quickly as I could.

'What's the urgent news,' I murmured wrapping the holey blanket around my shoulders.

'The Nazis. They're going to . . . ' he began but stopped as my bedroom door swung open. There stood Matron, rolling pin in hand. My fellow nurses were gathered behind, mouths agape in chock.

'Sister Newton! Sergeant Tennyson! What on earth is the meaning of this?'

11

I didn't know what to say. My reputation, such as it was, would now be in tatters. To my shock, Ray immediately took charge.

'Matron. Thank goodness. We had a report that Doctor Carr had been seen around the back of the Hall, trying to force windows.'

Matron lowered her rolling pin. 'Archie Carr. Impossible. He's hiding in . . . er . . . he'd never come back here.' She was quite flustered but recovered rapidly. 'Why are you in Sister Newton's bedroom? He's obviously not in here, Sergeant.'

'I heard a gasp from the Sister's room. The window was open, her light on and there was movement inside. I came in to check.'

I chose to add my two penneth. 'It . . . it was the nightingale. When I heard it, I wanted to see it. That's why the window was ajar.' It was the truth. Sort of.

'We heard the bird too, Matron. Just outside.' Nancy was backing me up as did the others. Matron wasn't convinced.

Ray pressed his advantage. 'Fetch Corporal Howard, one of you, nurses. He was the one who told me about the intruder.'

Ever suspicious, Matron nodded. 'You go, Nurse O'Rourke. And for heaven's sake cover yourself up. You'll give the unfortunate man a heart attack if he sees all that hanging out.'

Ray had the initiative now. He was so convincing even I believed him. 'Matron. Ladies. I'd hardly have a midnight assignation with Sister Newton dressed like this. See what I have here.' He fumbled in his trouser pocket causing a sharp intake of breath from two of the younger nurses before producing a small Webley revolver.

Brandishing it, he asked Matron if it was likely.

She shook her head. When the Corporal arrived, he had his own gun drawn. 'Did you catch him, Sergeant?' His was clearly on high alert, his eyes flicking all around as though he was searching for The Admiral.

'No,' Ray said angrily. 'And with all of this kerfuffle and commotion, he's legged it for sure. I hope you're pleased with yourself, Matron. And I believe you owe Sister an apology for jumping to conclusions.'

It was a masterful performance on his part, backed up no doubt by his pre-warned Corporal. From being my accuser, Matron was now on the defensive.

'My abject apologies, Sister Newton. I should never have doubted your integrity.'

★ ★ ★

It took a while before everyone returned to their beds. It was fortunate that the Sergeant was such a devious liar. I never did discover, what he had to tell me, though. As for him really planning anything intimate with me, I'm certain he understood me better than that. Anything more affectionate than a kiss would have to wait until we were finished with this mess at least. And it all depended on Ray. Considering the guilt that he felt, any advances had to come from him, whenever he was ready.

I saw Matron after brekkie and inquired if she still wished to share a promenade to the Cottage.

'Of course, Pauline. I am genuinely apologetic about my assumptions last evening. I've had a word with Sergeant Tennyson already. Shall we say eleven fifteen, after rounds?'

'I'll look forward to it, Blodwyn,' I replied. Perhaps she would open up to me about whatever was troubling her. In any case, it would be great to stretch my legs outside and check if I were back to my usual state of fitness.

When we both left, Sister Clara

Denmead was returning on that disgusting puke yellow bike of hers. Another visit to her Chorley relative no doubt. At least she could do that, whereas I was totally in the dark with my dad's op.

Ray Tennyson wasn't around in the building. I assumed he was coordinating the hunt for The Mastermind. He'd seemed very concerned about some meeting in Blackpool and was convinced that it might be a big target for the Axis infiltrators. The Lieutenant, his step-brother was running the hospital as efficiently as ever. We were lucky to have him. I had seen too many operations being run by those who had attained their rank by reasons of nepotism rather than ability, many often pressed to tie their own bootlaces.

The day was lovely. There was a sprinkling of swishing golden leaves still on the trees but winter was not far away. A squirrel scurried up an oak as we passed by on the leaf-covered pathway.

'The Lord of the Manor used to have shooting parties up in the lodge so it is . . . was, quite a grand two-storey building. Georgian, I believe, but I'm no expert on architecture. My dad was a coal miner. We were lucky to have a roof over our head, me and my kin.'

Although she was attempting to make conversation, Blodwyn's heart wasn't in it. I could tell. Whatever was on her mind was consuming her inside. What's more, I was certain it concerned that letter and her cryptic revelation that her hubby was alive.

She continued rabbiting on about everything mundane, avoiding topics which were contentious or close to her heart. Rain squalls were rolling in from the west and soon pewter-grey, billowing clouds swallowed the sun.

'This property of yours better be worth the trip, Blodwyn. Set in the woods? Makes it sound like a gingerbread house with a wolf or wicked witch lying in wait to pounce on unsuspecting children. You said it was abandoned, didn't you?'

She paused before answering. 'Not far, Pauline. Gone to rack and ruin but there are still some lovely features there. And the setting in spring with all the tulips and bluebells does give it a magical ambience. Apparently one of the previous Lords was as mad as a March hare. He built a labyrinth under the house and enjoyed listening to his guests try to escape. After a while, no one came to visit and he lost his mind altogether, the miserable, old wretch.'

'Charming,' I observed, shivering in the brisk breeze.

'There. That's it. You can see the chimney just above that laurel tree.' She pointed. 'Ready for an explore inside?'

'As I'll ever be.' Exploring dusty old houses wasn't high on my wishes list but Blodwyn and I had some bridge-building to do. She'd given me two photos of us with Nellie at Blackpool, one of which I'd posted to Oz. Whatever bonds we'd forged that day were sadly, long forgotten and that was a shame. Reaching the front door, I joked about wiping my feet before entering. She cracked a smile; the first I'd seen in quite a while.

Blodwyn produced a bulky key she used to unlock the entrance door with its intricate stained-glass panels.

Once we'd entered the foyer, I could see that it did have its own special character, a more rustic atmosphere than the Hall yet totally in sympathy to the forested setting. Dado and high picture rails separated the walls into three distinctive parts, yellowed paint delineating where pictures had once hung.

A boar's head gazed across the hall to that of a stag in a never-ceasing staring contest to see who would blink first.

In spite of being empty for decades, the air was permeated with tobacco smoke that lingered amongst the dampness of a place long since abandoned.

Reaching out, I swept a cobweb away, the sticky silken threads forming a thick strand which clung to my hand like a young possum to the back of its mother, afraid to let go. I wiped it on a torn curtain and moved warily forward.

'Spooky,' I commented. 'Good thing I don't believe in ghosts or superstitions.' For an unaccountable reason, I recalled the fortune teller and her reticence to predict my future. There was a joke my dad once told me about a doctor examining a patient and declaring that she didn't have long to live.

'Two or three years, doctor? One year then? No? How long? Tell me, please.'

'Let's put it this way, madam. I wouldn't buy a return bus ticket any longer.'

Although amusing at the time it wasn't now, either for my dad or for me. I'd almost died once in the past week. Maybe the grim reaper would be back again. Being in this derelict building wasn't such a good idea.

'I'm sorry. Blodwyn. I don't like it here at all. Can we go?'

I moved to retrace my steps as the

heaven's opened outside, flashes of lightning illuminating Blodwyn's sombre features.

'No, Pauline. I'm afraid you can't leave. I'm sorry.' Rolling thunder chased the lightning though my attention was solely on the woman I'd thought was my friend. She barred my way, before turning the key in the old mortice lock then dropping it down her blouse.

'This is not funny anymore, Blodwyn. Let me out this instant, or you and I are going to have a falling out, big time. I might not be one hundred per cent but you wouldn't stand a chance in hell once my dander is up.' I was fuming . . . and a little scared. What was going on with her? Had she lured me here? If so, for what? Somewhere secluded well away from the Hall.

Whatever it was, I'd had enough: I took one step forward and clenched my fist.

Blodwyn backed up until her back was against the dust-covered door.

I raised my fist but paused when I heard footsteps behind me.

'You're not going anywhere, Sister Newton. On the contrary, you and I are going to have one long discussion.'

I spun around. It was Archie Carr, a little worse for wear with stubble on his lean face.

'You're helping him?' I demanded of Blodwyn.

'It's not like that, Pau . . . ' she began before he cut her off.

'Yes. Matron is helping me and the cause of the Fatherland. She has no choice. Now, Matron. Give me the package you have for me. Schnell.'

Blodwyn hesitated before handing over a sealed box. Archie quickly tore off the wrapper, took out a gun from inside then finally discarded the brown container. My mouth opened in shock as did Matron's. She'd not realised what was in the box. Presumably, she'd been told to collect it then bring it here to Archie, along with me.

Worse still for me, was that the

revolver Archie had was levelled at my chest. He edged closer.

'As for why I asked her to bring you here, I thought it obvious. You're a spy; I'm a spy. And now you're going to tell me all that you know,' he sneered.

My mouth was dry and I had no chance to fight or flee. What on earth would happen when I told him the truth?

12

'I'm not a spy,' I said as forcefully as I could, considering he had a loaded gun aimed at me.

'You honestly expect me to believe that, Sister? I suspected you that first night, sent in to trip me up because your superiors suspected me and this Aussie accent. My chiefs thought it would be clever to masquerade as a colonial. When I heard you, I knew you'd catch me out, you or that little sneak Brenda. Well, she got her payback and soon it will be yours, too. But first I have to hypnotise you to learn all your secrets.'

This was maddening. 'I don't have any secrets you . . . you drongo.' I prayed that our Aussie impersonator was aware enough of Aussie slang to realise that 'drongo' was not a compliment.

Matron piped up, 'Maybe she's telling the truth, Doctor. I've found where they were hiding the Magna Carta for you and I've brought her here to you. Now I want you to release my husband, like you promised.'

So that was it. That letter with no stamp. Archie had given it to her, probably with proof that Elwyn was alive and in the custody of his Nazi collaborators, possibly right here in England. No wonder she had been behaving so oddly, searching the Hall too.

'All in good time, you fat, old bag. And just to clarify things; you don't tell me what to do. Otherwise, all I have to do is pick up this radio here and order my friends to kill your precious husband very, very slowly. It will be your fault, Matron. So near and yet so far.' He sniggered, leaning to one side.

From the way that he was standing, holding his injured arm, it was clearly giving him some jip. How rotten for him. Ray had told me they'd found a bunch of pain-killers in Archie's spartanly furnished room back at the Manor House.

'That bunged-up arm of yours, Doctor Carr? Was it really a German bullet that wrecked it up? I can't imagine you were shot by allies on the front line. You're too much of a coward to have been there. Stabbing a defenceless woman or a sleeping Doctor Allen is more your chicken-livered style.'

I realised that I was goading him and that he was armed and mad as a cut snake. Nonetheless. I was counting on him needing me to tell him all my secrets. The fact that I was totally not a spy wouldn't stop him from interrogating me but stalling for time was all I had up my linen sleeve. Trouble was, no one was aware we were out here in this dusty, dilapidated ruin.

'If you must be told the truth, Fräuline. It was I who shot myself in the arm. A wounded man is so much more easily accepted into your pathetic community of bleeding hearts, making my job as an infiltrator so much easier. No one would ever suspect me as a Nazi.'

I laughed out loud. Matron tried to shush my outburst but I wasn't going to let this little man intimidate me.

'Hah. You call yourself Das Genie . . . The Mastermind but to all of us, in Killymoor Hall, you were a joke.'

He stared at me, the gun wavering in his hand. It's hard to hold anything heavy for long and Archie wasn't a well man.

'You think I'm Das Genie, Fräuline? Interesting. But a joke. You're lying. I'm aware that your colleagues call me The Admiral behind my back? An Admiral is someone to be respected, like your one-armed Admiral Nelson. They call me that out of deference to my commanding stature.'

'Crikey, you pathetic little worm. They don't call you that because you remind them of Nelson. You shot yourself in the arm to gain credibility and as a subterfuge, probably damaging it for life. Was it meant to be a flesh wound that would get better?'

I saw the truth flicker across his eyes.

'Hah! It was. You couldn't even get that right. You're pitiable . . . a living, walking dingbat. They call you The Admiral as a shortened moniker for The Admiral of the Swiss Navy. You. Doctor Archie Carr.'

We watched as the truth filtered through his tiny brain. The Nazi's pale face suddenly flushed with anger, his sickly eyes opening wide as his self-control boiled away like water on a hot griddle. Archie moved closer, his lips quivering as he slowly pressed the gun barrel against my body so hard, I had to breathe in to reduce the pressure.

Slowly as though he were fighting to control his emotions, he whispered, 'You push me too much, Fräuline. If all Australian women are as arrogant and rude as you, I thank Der Führer that I am a true Aryan. At least in my homeland, the women keep their place.'

Then he backed away, allowing me to breathe again.

'What do you have to say for yourself now, Sister? Apologise, this instant.'

'You do realise you stink more than a pen of pigs, Admiral. The Master Race should learn to use soap now and again.' Damned if I were going to let him make me cower. I had no doubt he'd kill me eventually, probably the Matron and her hubby too once they'd outlived their usefulness. I was surprised Matron believed they'd both walk away from this but then I grasped she had someone else in her life she was trying to protect. Wouldn't I do the same if Ray were the one being held prisoner?

Archie stepped forward again just as the walkie-talkie whatsit made a squawky sound.

Archie paused, glaring' at me intently before placing the gun into his almost useless hand to answer the call. He spoke in German, seemingly elated at the news he heard. I was impressed with the quality of the sound. German engineering was so superior to our own in a lot of ways.

The message was from nearby, presumably on a frequency that our boys didn't suspect or monitor. Either that or it was being scrambled in some way that meant it was secure from evesdroppers.

Of course, it was all in German with its complicated multi-syllabled words. A few words sounded like English ones but to most people, the German lingo was gibberish, sounding just like a posse of turkeys gossiping.

Archie must have said the German equivalent of 'Roger, over and out' because he flipped a switch on the gadget and gave a malicious smirk.

'That was my colleague. We are ready to embark on the culmination of our glorious scheme; one that will give the whole of Britain the shock of their miserable little lives. After tonight's fireworks, they will quiver at the mention of the name Nazi. We will have destroyed one of their most important bases, killed politicians and generals and stolen your vaunted Magna Carta from the place your leaders chose to hide it. Not that either of you ladies will be alive to see it. Or your weak husband, Matron, I might add.'

'But you . . . you promised.' Matron was suddenly frantic. I placed a hand on her shoulder to gently restrain her.

'Hah. A promise to a woman? You are so gullible, Matron. We now have the Magna Carta and have no need of any information that you, Sister Newton, might have had. As of now, you are both . . . how do they say? 'Surplus to requirements'? I shall join my team using the car I've stolen and rendezvous with Das Genie . . . '

'What?' I blurted out. 'You're not the Mastermind?' I'd been wrong. 'No, of course, you're not. Too dumb by half. Someone else killed Doctor Allen. Your boss. Why did they murder him?'

'He suspected we were imposters and wrote a letter to the Ministry. I saw him writing his note and the rest is history, you stupid Sister. As for trying to delay me any further? Forget it. Your Australian cavalry won't be riding in to save you.'

'You really are an absolute dill, Doctor. The cavalry is American, not Australian. How did you ever graduate spy school?'

That did it. He flung the radio to one side, shattering the valves inside. As he attempted to change the revolver to his good hand, I barrelled into him with all my strength, Matron hitting out at him as well.

'Help!' I heard Matron yell as I struggled to wrest the weapon from Archie. He shoved me aside, forcing me to lose my balance as I fell, sprawling onto the carpeted floor. I saw him compose himself and lift the gun before a door behind him crashed open and all hell broke loose. Two soldiers barged into the room, disarming the startled doctor in a flash.

They restrained him, ignoring his

barrage of insults both in English and German. Eventually, he accepted his fate, glaring at Matron. 'It was you, wasn't it? Stitched me up, you lying, filthy traitor.'

Matron walked over to give him a slap across the face. 'You should talk. You were going to kill us all. I hope we can still save my Elwyn. At least, I know that you'll hang.'

'We?' he asked.

Ray walked in, searching through Archie's case full of documents he'd obviously discovered elsewhere in the house. 'Sorry we were late, Matron. Problems at the Hall; my brother and a few others injured. Seems like you ladies were managing quite well without us.'

Matron spluttered. 'I beg your pardon, Sergeant. He was about to shoot us, thank you very much.'

'With this?' Ray picked up the weapon that had so recently been pointed at my head. He aimed it at the ceiling and squeezed the trigger. There was a resounding click but nothing else; no falling plaster or loud bang, just a click.

'Not that I realised that you were giving him a revolver, Matron, yet it seemed only prudent to check your possessions after you told me about meeting The Admiral here. I took the liberty of removing the bullets.'

'I'm . . . I had no idea it was a gun, Sergeant,' Matron stammered. 'I was told it was medication. That's all.'

'It's a good thing, I'm far more suspicious than you then. We have Das Genie in custody now and that's all down to you being brave enough, Matron. You have done a great thing helping to capture Archie. I can only pray that we can rescue your husband. We'll make Archie talk, one way or another.'

My head was spinning. I had no idea what was going on. Unseen by everyone else, our German spy slowly took something from his pocket and was about to swallow it when I whacked his hand hard. A capsule clattered to the wooden boards on the edge of the carpet.

Archie screamed in frustration as Ray retrieved the object with his hanky. Examining it, he proclaimed it was a cyanide capsule. Archie had tried to take his own life rather than be interrogated, put on trial and no doubt executed for all sorts of war crimes.

'Take him next door, cuff him and make him comfortable. I'll be in soon. If he gives you any trouble, shoot him in the arm. The other one.' Archie suddenly became very quiet and complacent, avoiding any eye contact with the determined Sergeant. I was seeing another side of Ray now, a side I didn't particularly like. I hated this war for what it did to good men like Ray and to people like me and Matron.

Ray led us ladies through to another room with a surprisingly orderly settee. It seemed that Archie, ever the fastidious cleaner, had tidied his hideaway up as well as he could. Pity he didn't cleanse himself at the same time.

'You two need to talk. Meanwhile, I have a date with Archie Carr or Mr Mastermind as he calls himself.'

I interjected to correct him. 'He's not Das Genie. He told us. Das Genie has the Magna Carta and there's something big happening tonight. What did he say, Blodwyn? 'Destruction of a crucial base murdering politicians and generals'?'

Blodwyn nodded weakly. I was sure her mind was intent on saving her husband and time was wasting. But firstly, we had to discover where he was imprisoned.

'If he's not The Mastermind, then who?'

'No idea, Sergeant,' I replied. 'You . . . you're not going to torture Archie, are you?' Strangely, I was worried for the man who'd tried to kill me. No one deserved to be hurt like that, not even the impostor doctor.

Ray gave me a friendly smile. 'No, Pauline. But we are going to give him a taste of his own medicine . . . the same he used on our patients to extract information which he recorded in his notebook.' He took a vial and clean syringe from the Nazi's attaché case. 'I believe it's called sodium pentothal . . . truth serum.'

* * *

Interesting. It wasn't simply hypnosis The Admiral was using. Presumably, his victims had no knowledge of what he was doing to them in his 'relaxation therapy' sessions.

Once Ray had gone, that left Blodwyn and me alone, seated at opposite ends of the padded lounge suite. I glanced at the teapot and mugs on the polished table in front of us. Archie did enjoy his touches of luxury.

'Don't 'spose you fancy a cuppa?' I joked. It was an awkward moment for us both.

She broke out into a broad grin before resuming her ashamed expression.

'Pauline . . . ' she began then lapsed into silence once more, hunched over, staring abstractly at her fidgeting hands.

It was up to me.

'I don't blame you for what you did, Blodwyn,' I said gently reaching across to take her hands in mine. She drew them away, her face suddenly in front of mine.

'Well, you should . . . I betrayed you all, you, Sister Denmead, my nurses, the military. I helped them steal the Magna Carta for heaven's sake. It was only when I went to Lieutenant Tamara this morning to confess everything that I realised that I'm as big a traitor as any of them. Thank goodness, you weren't hurt.' Her voice was calmer by the end, tears welling and running over her cheeks.

I tried to reassure her, taking out a hanky and dabbing her eyes. 'Why didn't you tell me what you were doing on the way here?' She took my hand then, squeezing it with shaking fingers.

'It was the Sergeant. He said you

needed to react genuinely with Archie. I didn't have any idea about the gun.' She sat back to relate the sorry tale to me, the guilt which had been destroying her lovely nature now being shared in the expectation that I might understand.

I had been right about the envelope. There'd been a letter and large coloured picture in there. The Nazis did like to show off their expertise. Elwyn had been photographed with a copy of the Chorley Guardian to prove he was a prisoner nearby. How they'd managed to smuggle him into the country was beyond me. Submarine rather than parachute, I reckoned. Even so, they must have gone to a lot of trouble to enlist Matron's assistance in locating the Magna Carta.

'They let me speak to him on Archie's radio once,' she explained, her sobbing now under control. 'Just to keep me in check, I guess. It was heart-breaking. To think he's still being held by them is tearing me apart.'

'That radio Archie had? The range can't be too far. Can I have a look at that photograph of him, please?'

Blodwyn brightened up at my interest and produced a picture from her handbag.

I examined it closely as she leant across to point things out.

'He's still a handsome man, Blodwyn,' I commented, all the time scanning the surroundings to see if there were any clues as to where the photograph had been taken. It was outside under grey skies, a road and buildings visible behind him. There was a street sign but too indistinct to read. In addition, there was something strange Archie had said on the radio call. Some words in German.

'He has more grey hair and he's lost weight but he appears healthy enough, Pauline. And the clothes; they look new.' Elwyn wasn't smiling, despite it being normally a 'say cheese' situation when a snap was taken. Understandable, really. He'd realised he was a pawn in a scheme to blackmail his wife to do bad things but he couldn't escape.

'Could I borrow your glasses, please?' I inquired. Moving them back and forth revealed a bus on the edge of the photo passing by. It had livery on the side: 'Wright and . . . '

'What have you seen, Pauline? Do you know where he is? Sorry. Of course, you can't. You don't have a clue about the area around here.' Blodwyn's momentary elation vanished immediately. Her only hope in tracking down Elwyn's place of imprisonment lay with Ray and his interrogation of our infiltrator.

I had a question . . . one that had been there for quite some time. I had to ask.

'Blodwyn. You've kept the secret of this coercion by the Nazis quiet for days now. Furthermore, I realise they probably had you delivering food and drink to Archie here. Even with his stolen car, he'd hardly show his face outside or in a shop. Also, you've been spying on us and you found where they hid the Magna Carta. The one thing I need to hear from you is the reason you confessed all of this to Lieutenant and Sergeant.'

It took a long time for my friend to respond. It wasn't the reason, I suspected; it was the words to express her rationale. Eventually, she stood to pace around the tiny room, lifting the original photo that she'd shown me during those first few days of our friendship.

'It was last night; seeing you and Ray, pretending that you weren't in love. He was protecting your reputation with his well backed-up lies about searching for Archie. It was obvious they were lies. Archie was hiding here and wouldn't have been sneaking around the Hall. I've suspected you and the good Sergeant for a long time now; little nuances, looking the other way when you passed one another before a surreptitious peek when you believed no-one would notice.'

Blodwyn sat down by my side once more. 'You two have so much going for you as a couple yet you are both so unselfish, fighting to help others; Sergeant Tennyson on the train from Blackpool and you, putting your life in jeopardy to save Brenda. I mean she was hardly your best friend when you both arrived here.'

Her words caught in her mouth as she struggled to retain her composure. 'All last night, I tossed and turned, wondering why I was a traitor. Elwyn would sacrifice his life for others yet I wasn't strong enough. All I wanted to do was save him. That's when I resolved to come clean about my involvement to the authorities.'

She came towards me as I stood up. 'Pauline. I'm am so, so very sorry for what I've done to everyone, especially you. I put you in danger. If it hadn't been for the Sergeant emptying that gun . . .'

I took her in my arms, holding her

shaking body to mine. We remained there, me stroking her hair and repeating it would be okay. The truth was I had no idea if it would. She'd betrayed our trust and now England's founding document of history had been snatched and was in the hands of the most insidious evil the Empire had ever faced.

Would she be charged with treason? Would her husband be killed before we found him, wherever he was? I wished I could reassure her more.

* * *

Ray entered the room at that moment, Archie and the two soldiers with him. Archie was groggy but seemingly unhurt.

'Elwyn?' Matron asked, her expression hopeful that they'd learnt the location of her hubby.

Ray shook his head. 'The drug didn't work on him. I suspect secret agents like The Admiral have been versed in interrogation techniques. He mumbled some incoherent words then clammed up. Have we any clues at all as to where he might be imprisoned or what the group's target is for tonight?'

No one spoke until I did. 'The Chorley newspaper in the photograph and the fact Matron spoke to Elwyn on the radio suggests he's close by. Also, when Archie was on the radio to his superior, he told them he would see them at three o'clock. 'Sich in die Höhle des Löwen begeben'.

Archie immediately stirred, an expression of pure horror on his grimy, stubbled face.

'Himmels willen! You speak German?' He collapsed on to the floor in a heap, realising I'd understood his secret radio conversation.

'Wie ein Eingeborener,' I spat back at him. 'Like a native' was the translation although it wasn't strictly true. My grandmother was from Bavaria and I hadn't understood all that he'd spoken yet I was damned if I'd admit to that.

Ray and Blodwyn were as shocked as was Archie. 'You are full of surprises, Sister,' Ray conceded. 'You could have said.'

'Confessing to speaking German these days isn't always a good thing for one's health,' was my answer. 'You said so yourself, Sergeant.'

'What did he say to his cronies then, Miss Clever Clogs?' Ray said. 'Can it help us find Blodwyn's husband?'

I mused for a moment. 'It didn't make a great deal of sense to me but I'm hoping it will to you. He told them he'd meet them in the lion's den.' I was making a point of watching Archie for a reaction, as was Ray. Although the practised spy tried to conceal his emotions, we could discern that he was angry at himself for his inadvertent slip of the tongue.

Ray replied. 'There aren't many lions in Chorley or dens for that matter. However, British pubs are often called The Red Lion for some bizarre reason. Maybe because of the unicorn and lion on our coat of arms.'

I hadn't realised that. A mythical creature and an African big cat? Wouldn't a hedgehog and a fox be more appropriate? I tried to stop my mind digressing. Ray was examining the photograph for a sign of a pub. There wasn't any.

'There must be dozens of pubs with Lion in their name unless anyone can link the photo with a location?'

I'd already thought this through. 'I'm afraid I don't have any idea about Chorley at all but if I'm right, there is a bloke we can go to who knows the town like the back of his hand. Shall we go?'

'We?' was Ray's response.

'Sergeant Tennyson. From now on, I'm a part of your team whether you like it or not. I want to catch this Mastermind as much as you.'

Ray didn't argue which was a good sign for our future relationship. I was positive, there would be one, too.

'We'll need to call to the Hall first. I have to check on my brother and the others. Then we'll make our way to Chorley to track down Elwyn. May I ask who we'll be seeing, Pauline?'

I grinned and began to head for the front door with Blodwyn. 'A lovely, chubby and balding old man with his fleet of buses.'

13

Matron wanted to come too, understandably. However, we soon convinced her she was better helping at the hospital. Sister Denmead and a few other workers were missing, possibly injured by the attack this morning while Ray had been elsewhere. There was the possibility they'd been taken as hostages, a thought which further complicated our attempt to rescue Elwyn Jones.

It was fortunate that the attack on the Hall had been swift and precise. No one had been seriously hurt though Norman Tamara did have a nasty bump on the head which had required stitches.

When Matron and I entered the foyer, the large map of the Killymoor Hall estate was lying on the tiles floor in tatters, the frame broken. Norman

Tamara was there, a bandage on his temple and cuts across both cheeks.

'I'm so sorry I told them,' bemoaned Blodwyn, to us all.

'I don't understand,' I said before realising the truth. 'Oh. The Magna Carta was secreted at the back of the estate map, wasn't it?'

'Yes,' said Ray, not showing much concern. 'Hiding the document in plain sight wasn't a great idea. It's a good thing it was a fake; a good one designed to fool the thieves.'

We both stared at him and Norman in surprise.

'What? You don't think they'd entrust the real one to nobodies like us, do you? I can't even tie my shoelaces properly and my brother, Norman here, isn't much better.' Ray gave one of those sheepish grins that made him so engaging.

Norman Tamara took up the story. 'We were aware of an agent, based around the area and so, we concocted a trap to lure them in. Then I had Ray posted here as a humble Sergeant to work behind the scenes to sabotage the saboteurs. We've caught quite a few but the Mastermind literally evaded our grasp. We did suspect a number of workers here, including Captain Franciscus as well as Archie Carr.'

He stumbled and had to sit down on the marble stairs that swept up to the first floor. Matron, ever the caring professional, checked his pulse as he continued his story.

'In the end, we narrowed it down to The Admiral but we were wrong. He was just another minion. The real leader is still at large and plotting something catastrophic for tonight. Ray and his specialist team will try to catch them all at Chorley, rescue your husband, Blodwyn, and prevent them from carrying out their evil scheme.'

Blodwyn summoned a nurse to fetch a wheelchair before addressing the two of us.

'I think Lieutenant Tamara has done enough for today. That fight he was in has taken its toll. Some bed rest is in order. I'll look after him . . . That is if you're not going to have me arrested for what I've done, Sergeant.' She was clearly concerned about her future.

'Arrested? Whatever for, Matron? You were bravely acting on my orders to capture Archie Carr. Now I suggest you take care of my brother and the others. As for Elwyn, I promise to do my best to reunite the two of you.'

I don't know who was more surprised when my friend embraced Ray in her arms and kissed him on both cheeks. Me or Ray.

'You have a real gem there, Sister Newton. You two take care of one another.' With that, she and the returning nurse eased Norman into the wheelchair and left.

'What now, Ray?' I asked. He examined his watch. Twenty to two. Eighty minutes to arrive at the Lion's Den at the time Archie had arranged. We'd be pushing it.

Our belief was that Elwyn would be

safe until Archie arrived. It's what he'd instructed his fellow spies on the radio although I hadn't told Blodwyn as it was too upsetting. 'Keep the Welsh man alive,' he'd told them. 'I want to execute him myself after I gloat that I'd already shot his precious wife.'

Archie Carr deserved everything he'd get.

* * *

Whatever rank Ray really held must have been high. Within a few minutes, a squad of six commandos arrived already wearing civilian clothing. One handed Ray a package of civvies with a string holding the bundle together. We were seated in the back of an army transport truck.

'Thank you, Sub-Lieutenant,' said Ray. I raised an eyebrow. I'd assumed they were army yet the rank of his second in command was naval. This was a select group of the military. The officer saluted him and re-joined his

264

colleagues who were checking their handguns and other items.

I did realise the need for their covert disguise. Approaching the nest of Nazis in hiding, whilst dressed as soldiers, would be stupid. Two were sporting wigs of grey hair and false beards.

'What about my disguise?' I asked.

'What you wore for your stroll this morning is fine. They won't suspect a woman, Pauline. We'll do a recon of the area then you'll stay somewhere safe when we make our move. Besides, I didn't think you would want to be changing in front of these red-blooded young men.'

They all smiled and I heard one mutter, 'Spoilsport'. Then I recognised him. He was an orderly at the hospital. And another was one of Cook's assistants.

Ray turned his back on me to change, dropping his trousers. I tried to look away but the scar from shrapnel was quite prominent. Then with his shirt off, it was evident how many wounds he'd sustained and had patched up, some not very neatly.

I must have gasped. His eyes met mine. 'Not one of your pretty movie stars, I'm afraid. Sorry, you had to see that.' He buttoned up his shirt and donned a baggy jumper with deep pockets.

'Not a big fan of them, apart from *Lassie,*' was my reply. I'd keep my other reassurances until later. 'How long until we're at the bus depot?'

The guy seated next to the driver opened the tarp between us and announced. 'Just around the corner, Sister.' His wide grin belayed the astonishment on my face. It was the Private I'd thrown out for his attitude when I'd first arrived.

'Didn't recognise you with your clothes on, Private,' I joked. It was finally clear to me why a healthy young bloke was in the hospital; Ray was rotating them through the employees and patients as a subterfuge to flush out information about Das Genie.

'No problems, Sister. Good to see you again. And it's actually Warrant Officer . . . for the record.'

★ ★ ★

Mr Wright was awaiting us all, ushering us inside via a rear-entry door.

Ray didn't mess around with preliminaries. The owner had been briefed to expect us on a matter of national security.

I laid out the photo next to the town plan of Chorley, already on his large desk. Recognising me and Ray, he listened. The remainder of the commando team milled around, being as inconspicuous as they could. It was difficult. The only young able-bodied men in England these days were few and far between. They weren't built like brick dunnies either, unlike these.

I explained the reference to the 'lion's den' and showed him the photograph. He quickly named two of the buildings in the background as being in the north-western industrial part of the town.

'And that bus is a double-decker. Not a lot of routes for that, with too many low railway bridges. That's where I believe it is; on Stump Lane,' he tapped his stubby finger on the map.

'And what about the Lion reference?' I said, pushing him. Time was running out.

He put his hand to his chin before exclaiming. 'That must be it; the White Lion. Not a nice pub, Sister. Lots of scallywags and low-lives. Yeah. That'd be it. No other Lion pubs near there.' He checked his watch. 'The two twenty-six goes by there. It'll take seven minutes or thereabouts. Why don't you and your lot hop a ride on my bus and arrive inconspicuous, like? Jump off the stop before and after, here and here.'

'Makes sense, boss,' the second in command said. 'We can arrive like coming home from a shift.'

Ray nodded.

'And you two can pretend to be a

married couple, going for a drink. Just make sure your missus don't open her mouth. That accent of hers would be a dead give-away.'

The banter belied the tension. It was going to be nasty going up against all those armed Germans.

★ ★ ★

The short bus journey was quiet. The owner drove, indicating where we each should get off. Some of Ray's men had work bags as though they had just finished and were stopping off for a drink on the way home. The pub shouldn't have been open at this time but a lot of rules were overlooked because of the war.

Ray and I left the bus and ambled along towards where the rendezvous destination was, behind some derelict factories. We walked arm in arm as we were supposed to be sweethearts out for a stroll and a drink. The few minutes alone gave us a chance to think.

'Pauline, I have something to confess.' Ray was uncomfortable. Still, I suspected it was the conversation with me rather than the imminent incursion into the den of Nazis.

'My goodness, Ray. If I look like a Catholic priest to you, you really do need some glasses.'

He gave a sardonic smile but at least it was a smile. 'Blodwyn said something this morning that made me understand love in a way which I'm afraid I'd forgotten. She was talking about Elwyn, explaining why she'd betrayed us, as she had. Sometimes logic isn't enough to justify what we do. I'm . . . I'm sorry. I'm not good with words and feelings. Guess I've been so busy repressing my emotions, I can't recognise them when they sneak in another way.'

I squeezed his hand with mine, sensing his warmth and the leaves nearby moving gently in the cool wind. 'Take your time,' I whispered, conscious that we were coming up to the entrance. He stopped, glancing around. We still had fifteen minutes until the arranged time Archie would be met inside.

Two of Ray's squad passed by, ignoring us as they joshed about some fictitious incident at their equally fictitious workplace. When it came to acting, they were good. They walked inside the White Lion as yet another operative came from the other end of the street, stopping to light up a cigarette.

He was checking the lie of the land and would probably remain outside to keep an eye on comings and goings. Surprisingly, he had a dog on a rope with him. Where had he found that?

'I love you. You do realise that. And I believe you love me too, despite my less than perfect body.'

'I do love you, Ray,' I confirmed, thinking how long I'd waited to hear that from him.

'The trouble was, Pauline, there were all these other things rattling around inside my head; my wife and children, the danger I'm in doing this job, the lies

I tell about who I am and what I do. And then there's the future . . . '

He glanced around again before facing me, tucking that wayward strand of my mousey brown hair under my scarf before caressing my cheek with his rough fingertips.

'Blodwyn said it. 'We have to embrace whatever love we can find here and now.' She was so right. I comprehend that now. The past is gone, finished . . . leaving us with our memories and little else. The future . . . well, we don't know but the present . . . '

He leant forward to touch his lips to the tip of my nose then, ever so hesitantly, he moved them lower to press against mine. I breathed in the warmth and passion then returned his expression of love as ardently as I could, reaching my arms around to hug his body to mine.

We only moved apart when some elderly women expressed their disgust at such overt affection in public. We both smiled at that.

'Time to have a drink, darling?' Ray announced loudly, in order to continue our deception.

The interior of the pub stank of stale beer, staler smoke and people. A grey cloud suffused the air and fabric of every part of the seedy establishment. The curtained, leaded windows and dingy lighting didn't help.

Never having adopted the habit of smoking, despite its popularity with the movie set, I found the stink offensive and daintily lifted a hanky to hold to my delicate nosey. What was more, we were getting a lot of nasty stares.

'Sweetheart. Can we not go elsewhere? The smoke does so bring tears to my eyes,' I said in a rather good London accent.

'Just one drink, my love. After that, we shall go.' His own accent mirrored mine. 'Barkeep? A glass of your finest bitter for me and a sherry for my fiancée.'

'We don't serve ladies in here,

mister,' was the burly man's curt reply. True, it was unusual in Australia, women being confined to the more genteel setting of the Ladies' Bar, but I thought conventions were more relaxed in Britain. Obviously not.

I indicated the women sitting around the room, some on men's laps. They all had a glass. 'What about them?' I asked, politely.

The barkeeper laughed heartily, his missing teeth evident as he did so. 'They ain't no ladies.'

I feigned shock at the inference. 'Goodness me. 'Tis all right, Raymond. I shall have a cup of Earl Grey later.'

We sat at a none-too-clean table, me showing my dislike for being here every so often as my insensitive 'boyfriend' persisted on enjoying his drink by sipping it slowly as I sat there fuming. If anyone were watching, I was making it obvious that I wasn't happy being dragged in here.

Ray's men were mingling, awaiting the appearance of the bloke meeting

Archie. Three o'clock came and went without anyone else entering. Then, as we were all becoming concerned that he may have been scared off, a young man arrived.

His eyes darted everywhere. He was searching for Archie, I assumed, and was getting edgy not seeing him here as arranged. Then his eyes locked on me. I could feel it. Was he wondering what I was doing here? I pouted, before sitting back, crossing my legs under the dress.

It wasn't enough and Ray sensed it too. All of a sudden, he stood up and leant over to kiss me very forcefully. I pushed him off and slapped him. Hard. 'How dare you, Raymond! Can't you see I don't want to be here?'

The whole pub had ceased talking, staring at us. I flounced my dress up to cover my bodice and began to sob.

Ray made a show of begging for forgiveness and calming me down. I figured our spy would hardly believe that a hysterical woman would be a threat. I was right. When I next peeked, he had dismissed me.

He approached an unassuming older bloke near us who shrugged and declared that the doctor hadn't arrived yet. Then they both went outside, heading across the road. Ray didn't have to instruct anyone to follow them. His team were professionals.

Trying to avoid it appearing that we were pursuing them, we waited a few minutes with me continuing to glower. Eventually, I stood and told Ray we'd stayed long enough.

'Haven't finished my drink yet, sweetie,' he protested, making no effort to move. I stamped my feet, picked up his glass and threw the remaining contents over his face.

'Well, you have now, Raymond. And as for us, we're finished too.' I stormed out in the biggest huff I could manage, leaving a room full of cheering and clapping men.

As I opened the door, I heard the bartender say, 'Best go after her, mate.

Otherwise no how's-your-father for you tonight.'

Performance almost over, I made a show of waiting impatiently as Ray came out appearing decidedly soggy. He was pleading for me to forgive him. All the time I was peering up and down the street. There, to the left and a good few hundred yards away, I saw one of the squad head down a side street.

We headed that way, stopping when I saw a bicycle leaning against an abandoned building in the distance.

'Oh crikey,' I exclaimed. Facing Ray, I pointed out the bike.

'Terrible choice of colour. Yukky yellow. So what?'

'It's Sister Denmead's.'

Ray stared at me, the implications quickly sinking in. 'What you said, Pauline. 'Crikey',' he agreed. All of those trips to visit her crook relative were a lie.

By now the few of his team whom I could see were armed and moving in on the boarded-up warehouse which our suspects had entered.

Ray took me by both shoulders. 'Right, Pauline. You stay here, under-cover and well hidden. I do not want you getting shot.'

I gave him a kiss, momentarily wondering why he was so wet. Then I remembered.

'Believe it or not, my hero, I don't want me being shot either. Or you for that matter.'

I crouched down behind a rusting truck that was clearly going nowhere, peeking around the corner of the broken headlight to watch as the group converged on the three shuttered doors. There was a big set of two large doors also that were for vehicular traffic in and out. They were padlocked shut with a chain.

Within moments, the men had all vanished. Shouts and two gunshots made dull sounds from inside. I hardly dared breathe. The nearby streets were deserted and I realised the saboteurs had chosen here to conceal their comings and goings.

Presumably, Archie hadn't been here before and only knew the White Lion pub as a meeting place so that he could be led here without attracting too much attention. Archie wandering up to a group of British soldiers and asking the way to the nearest Nazi hiding place probably wasn't in his *How to Be a Successful Spy* instruction book.

One of the side doors opened at last and the youth I'd seen searching for Archie came out. My whole body went cold and tensed. At that moment, I realised his hands were behind his back. Ray emerged, holding a weapon on the Axis agent. Two other handcuffed members of the cell emerged and then an older man, supported by two English commandos. It must have been Elwyn.

Ray waved me over to join them. By this time the German trio were on their tummies, feet also bound. Ray's team were taking no chances. Three others came from the building.

'All clear boss. The rest must have

already gone. We'll start processing the site.'

Police and other military personnel were soon arriving by trucks and cars. I assumed they'd been summoned by radio once the Ratzis had been subdued. From the sound of it, they'd not put up much resistance. The raid by Ray's men had been swiftly executed. Simply put, they'd been caught with their pants down.

The grey-haired soldier's face was gaunt yet he retained a gleam of defiance in his bloodshot eyes. There were no visible wounds yet his demeanour and emaciated body showed how poorly he'd been treated as a prisoner-of-war.

Ray introduced us. 'Lance-Corporal Jones. This is Sister Pauline Newton. She's a friend of your lovely wife and has helped my team locate you.'

He reached out to take my hands in his. The physical weakness couldn't hide an underlying strength.

'Thank you,' he said in his lilting Welsh accent.

'She's Australian,' Ray continued.

'Oh, I shall not hold that against you, my dear. We all have our crosses to bear,' he commented with a wink, giving my hand an extra squeeze. I heard an ambulance bell clanging and saw it heading our way.

As they bundled him into the back, Ray explained to him that he was being taken to Matron at Killymoor Hall. 'She's been told you're safe and sound and will be with you soon. I believe she has a message for you. There's something called Barrow Brith? And she has some especially ready for you.'

'Bara brith, sir. It's a cake from God's own country. My favourite. I hope to see you both later.' Although he wasn't in uniform, Elwyn Jones clearly understood that Ray was in charge of the assault team and should be addressed as such.

'You will, Lance-Corporal, you will,' Ray replied. They closed the ambulance doors and headed off leaving us with the three prisoners and a huge puzzle to solve and just a few hours to do it in.

Where were Sister Clara Denmead and her cronies and could we stop them in time?

14

Ray's friendly attitude and our relief at saving Matron's hubby was set aside as he gave commands to his team and to others who'd come. One newly-arrived officer stupidly asked why Ray behaved like he was in charge. Ray took out some sort of card from his pocket and flashed it at the officious soldier. The Second Lieutenant immediately stood to attention and saluted before relaying Ray's commands to everyone else.

'I'd like a phone connection set up inside and a high-powered two-way radio as well as an operator. Also, these three Germans must be searched and questioned. I'm guessing they won't be privy to the master plan. These cells operate on a need-to-know basis. They'll still be shot as spies.' His comments were made in close proximity to the three prostrate prisoners.

'Ixnay. I'm not German. I'm English,' claimed the young man from the pub.

'I'm sorry. I didn't realise,' Ray commented, kneeling by his side. Then he stood and instructed the guard with the gun. 'I want this man processed differently, Sergeant. He's British. Therefore, he'll be hanged first for being a traitor then shot as a spy.'

The youth tried to jump up but was shoved back down by a boot. 'What? Hold on. I didn't realise. They told me they were Polish black-marketeers.'

'And the fact that they spoke German didn't make you at all suspicious?' Ray suggested, sarcastically.

'Polish? German? Welsh, like that man we had locked up? It's all the same to me. I can't even talk English proper. Bloody foreigners.' He was only a teenager. The promise of a few shillings and he would have jumped at the chance to help them. I figured he was employed for his local knowledge.

Ray was genuinely angry. 'Your

so-called Polish mates blew up an ammo depot a few weeks ago. And tried to derail a train. You must have suspected?'

'Me? No? Honest. I didn't think it were them for one minute.' He seemed genuinely shocked.

Ray addressed the soldiers standing guard. 'Keep him here. He might be useful. You can take the others away. I don't think they have any info they'll tell us anyway. Expendable. Probably just here to kill the man they were supposed to meet so that he wouldn't talk if captured.'

Kill Archie? But he was one of theirs. It was at that moment I realised that Ray understood the mind of our enemy far better than I did. To execute one of their own was unthinkable.

'Come on, Pauline. I want you inside to see what we can ascertain about their intended target.' Ray took my hand and led me to the now open side door nearest us. People were running back, and forth in all directions. Just then, two blokes pulled open the garage doors, presumably to allow more light into the viper's nest from where our enemies had planned their subterfuge and attacks.

'Why me? I'm just a nurse. I don't comprehend any of this.' Despite Ray being with me, I was a little afraid. The adrenalin of the pub charade had worn off. I'd already had a gun pointed at me once today by that vicious Archie and I was still weak from that blood transfusion.

All that walking this morning and now. I felt like crawling into my bed at Killymoor Hall and closing my little eyes. All of this . . . this unbelievable madness . . . it wasn't for me.

Ray paused. 'Pauline. I do understand that I'm asking a lot from you. This isn't your world at all. You save lives and sadly, sometimes I have to take them. I'm not asking you to tag along only because I love you or that you're a gorgeous morale booster for all my men. You're here because I trust you and that incisive mind of yours. You can perceive things that the rest of us can't.'

'Well,' I replied, rapidly recovering my energy after that pep-talk, 'When you put it so nicely, how can I refuse to help?'

We entered the large, open structure. There appeared to be a few rooms in the back but most of it looked like a base of operations for about a dozen men. Their unmade bunks were on the right near a makeshift kitchen and some toilet and washing facilities that were thankfully hidden behind a closed door. It was a shame that the odour could still be smelt though, in spite of the outside doors being wide open.

'Where shall we start?' Ray asked.

'That table over there near the wall with maps. I'm guessing they took what they needed but there might be some discarded notes in the bin. They didn't expect us here, remember.'

As we went across, Ray called out to check everywhere for an indication of their proposed target and how they could bypass security. It was evident that they'd be hitting a high-profile and securely protected site.

'What a mess. You'd think if Sister Denmead was involved, she would have at least tidied the place up, Pauline.' I wasn't sure if it was Ray's humour or not.

'Not all women are domestic goddesses, Ray. I'm not. In fact, back in Wagga, the fire brigade turns up whenever I try to cook. As for Clara Denmead, I don't believe her role was to clean or to please men in other ways. Think about it. Archie couldn't have killed Doctor Allen; you said so yourself. I reckon Clara Denmead is Das Genie.'

Ray considered that momentarily. 'A woman? But it makes sense. Any clues as to what she might be planning?'

I was surprised he'd accepted my suggestion so readily. Like all good leaders, he wasn't one to pretend he had all the answers. He listened to others before committing. By this time, we'd reached the wall with maps and plans. Some were printed, others painstakingly sketched by hand with a scale denoting distances. Yet, even with my knowledge of German, the printed notations made little sense.

'Maybe this is a fuel depot just here, perhaps.'

A private came running across, brandishing some paperwork. 'One of the local residents mentioned a bus leaving this street but not one of Mr Wright's fleet. It was navy blue and we've found spray cans with that colour over there.' He pointed. 'Also, a report of a large truck stolen yesterday ties up with tyre marks on the floor.'

'We need a blackboard to collate this information, Ray. And that English lackey from outside. He might be able to . . . ow!' I'd kicked something hard so bent down to check what. A discarded wooden hanger was under some newspapers. There was a label on it from a local dry-cleaners. The address was easy enough to read.

'Ray. Can we have someone phone this laundry to check on anything unusual happening recently? Clothing being stolen, perhaps?' I handed him the hanger. He instructed one of his own men to do that.

Making certain we were out of earshot of the others, I asked him if there were anything top-secret happening tonight in the area, possibly involving politicians. A meeting possibly. I didn't want details. These days secrets were meant to be exactly that.

'There's nothing. I half wish there were, Pauline. Then we'd at least be able to intercept them.'

There had to be. Archie boasted about it and about the time for the fireworks. Eight pm. How in the name of all that was holy they'd managed to discover the when and where was beyond me but they were a resourceful bunch and adept at infiltration and gathering supposedly inviolate information.

'Do me a favour. Contact your boss.

Contact Mr Churchill himself but double-check with someone. This nest of Nazis is burning its bridges, exposing the identities they've spent months setting up. Stealing the Magna Carta is only part of this operation. A dozen highly trained saboteurs and spies do not risk everything so that they can take a drive in the countryside.'

'You're right. It doesn't make sense. You'll have to excuse me. I've got a radio call to make.'

He left me to deal with the young local man. Two guards dragged him in, not being too polite about it. They dumped him at my feet.

Despite all of the drama and threats about being shot as a traitor, he was still blasé enough to make a comment about my legs.

I hitched up my frock a little to show my calves. 'Take a good look, mate. You won't be seeing any woman ever again. What's more, I'm the only thing standing between you and a whole lot of pain before you meet your maker.

You are a traitor and that German woman giving the orders threw you and your Nazi mates to the wolves. You need to start talking. No. Actually, you need to start singing ... just like a nightingale. And you have thirty seconds to start.'

* * *

By the time Ray returned, I'd written a few more items on the blackboard which had been discovered. My boyfriend was livid.

'You were absolutely right, Pauline. Some sort of communication cock-up, pardon my French. I should have been told.'

He smashed his open palm down on the tabletop in frustration, wincing a little from the pain. I'd never seen him this angry, really angry. He was breathing too quickly and wouldn't be thinking straight.

'Some water for him, please,' I asked one of his team. By this time Toby, the young sympathiser, had been taken away to a detention cell elsewhere. He'd not told us much as he hadn't understood most of what had been said. In truth, he'd only heard what they wanted him to hear. We now had a definite figure of the number involved. Ten plus the two men who'd already been captured here in this building. Oh, and let's not forget Sister 'butter-wouldn't-melt' Denmead.

However, he had described some observations he'd made concerning their behaviour when they were relaxing.

And, to me, it made absolutely no sense at all.

Nevertheless, it was up there on the blackboard with two question marks next to it.

'Take a moment to compose yourself, Sergeant,' I whispered to him, 'Everyone here needs you to be focused and in control. You're the one giving orders. Remember?'

He smiled, took a deep breath and a

sip of the proffered water. 'I want everyone to come here, thank you. We don't have a lot of time before the Nazis are going to strike.'

'Boss,' said his next in command. 'Are you sure you want everyone to hear this? There's the matter of clearance and . . .'

'I appreciate what you're saying number two but if the Germans already have every detail about this clandestine meeting then I can't see the point of hiding it from our own countrymen. Hell. We may even take out a full-page advertisement in the papers. There's a mole very high up in our government, I'm ashamed to say.'

He waited until the investigators were gathered around, waiting impatiently.

'The Nazis are headed to Blackpool in a painted blue bus. There's a high-level war cabinet meeting involving politicians and military planners from all over the Empire, including your country, Pauline. Us Brits will host it. Not sure if Winnie himself might be there.' Ray took a deep breath. 'It is my belief our Nazi friends will infiltrate the aircraft base and attempt to assassinate the delegates.'

There was a collective gasp followed by murmurings of disbelief.

'We need to discover how they will carry out this plan. I want to hear all that you fellows have discovered. Now, please and one at a time.'

Someone put their hand up. 'There were twenty blue dress uniforms stolen from a dry-cleaners. Sister Newton found a coat-hanger from there.'

Two others offered information about poorly counterfeited documents found in rubbish bins two blocks away. They were for British air force personnel.

I piped up next. 'The English youth told us the Nazis were playing musical instruments a lot. Seems strange if you're trained killers.' Then I put a connection to the shreds of clues. 'Not so much if you're pretending to be a band invited to the big-wigs get-together.'

Ray stared at me making the same conclusion. 'That's it, Pauline . . . everyone. Somehow, they've wrangled an invite or will intercept the genuine band to gain entrance through the high-security guards at the base. I just hope we're in time. My squad? We move out in five. Where's my radio operator?'

I checked one of the men's watch. It would be getting dark outside.

I added one more observation as the strike team of Ray's started to mobilise. 'There's another fact, sir. That wideboy. He said they painted an 'X' on the side of that truck they stole.'

Ray paused, unsure if this was relevant. 'An 'X'; like in 'X marks the spot'?'

'I guess,' I replied, wondering if I should have probed for more information.

Ray decided he'd worry about it later. He took the radio microphone and began to make a call. I turned to go. I'd get a lift back to the Hall with some of the other people here. It was high time to check on Elwyn.

'Pauline. Wait. Where do you think you're heading?' Ray asked, his hand over the microphone.

'The Hall. I'm no use here.' I'd done my bit . . . or so I thought.

'You're needed with us. You might understand the way Sister Denmead thinks . . . certainly far more than I can. Besides. You speak German.'

I could see he had more important things to do than argue with me. In any case, he'd keep me out of harm's way just as he'd done when they'd raided this place.

'Okay,' I answered, returning to his side. Another visit to Blackpool might be interesting although I doubted that I'd have the chance for any fairy floss this time.

* * *

Much longer than five minutes later, we were back in what Ray called his 'battle truck'. His team were with us again, chatting and checking weapons as only professionals would do on their way to another encounter with the enemy. I assumed that they each had their own set of specialised skills.

I felt totally out of place, them all now in their regulation uniforms of dark camouflage colours with leather boots and me in my brightly decorated floral frock with a thick woolly turquoise jumper. Talk about not dressing for the occasion.

'Listen up men . . . and woman. I had the devil's own time getting through to anyone with clout. Then I had to deal with self-important officers too afraid to make a decision of their own or, if they could, then they were so arrogant as to believe that no one could get past their security. All that time wasted. Finally, I managed to speak to a Wing Commander who was privy to my code name. He actioned my suggestions immediately although he couldn't believe they could be that audacious. Let's be hopeful that they weren't too late.'

'Have to agree with him, sir. It takes some . . . you know what, to drive right into an air force base, pretend that you're a band, then start shooting. It's a suicide squad.'

He was dead right. I remembered Archie saying 'into the lion's den'. Maybe it had an additional meaning to The White Lion pub.

We were speeding along and this old truck didn't have good suspension. Hitting a big bump, we all lurched from one side to the other, me falling into the arms of the soldier next to me.

'Sorry,' I said.

'Any time, Sister,' was his light-hearted reply. 'On second thoughts, my apologies. There's no way that I want to be on the receiving end of that hay-maker slap you hit the boss with in the pub. Are all you Aussie women that truculent?'

Ray spoke up in the defence of my countrywomen. 'No, Steve. My Pauline is a definite one-off.' That caused an outburst of laughter in the group. It was clear this squad of Ray's were trained professionals used to covert ops and working together. Rank wasn't necessarily mentioned but they all kept their place and trusted one another.

I had to ask. 'So why are we racing over there? Presumably the military over there has the situation in hand.'

'Because, my dear Pauline, we can identify their ringleader, Sister Denmead. If she isn't on the bus but gets into the base, she could cause untold havoc. After all, who would suspect a woman? We didn't. Also, I've been thinking about the truck they stole, the one with the 'X' on the sides. Sister Clara wouldn't have stolen it for no reason.'

I nodded, trusting the driver and navigator to get us to Blackpool in one piece. All of these pot-holes and being tossed around like a rag doll? My stomach wasn't coping well, at all. I needed something solid to rest against and so pressed up to Ray's side. When he gave me a quizzical glance, I discreetly reminded him of our meeting in the forest and that he didn't object to being close to me then. Unfortunately, my whispered words must have been heard by the others who sniggered and asked for details. How embarrassing! Bored, I decided to peruse the maps of the base, making sure I hid my face between the others with the plan, using the dull interior lights as well as I could. Blackpool Air Base couldn't come fast enough.

★ ★ ★

'We're here, boss,' the navigator announced, not before time.

The jovial attitude was muted now. Ray's squad were in readiness for whatever would be required of them. Words were exchanged at the sentry point but, trapped in the tomb-like enclosed rear of the truck with two rows of soldiers facing one another, we couldn't make out the conversation.

Then the rear flap of the truck was tugged back allowing a uniformed officer to examine us as occupants.

'Who's in charge here?' he inquired briskly, vaulting up inside. The truck began moving, following directions of another base airman who'd climbed into the cab.

'I am, Wing Commander. Was it you I spoke to?'

'Yes, sir. It was a close call but we got them all. Ten men pretending to be band members from Manchester. Bloody good counterfeit IDs too. Pardon my language, ma'am.'

'Any casualties?' Ray said.

'No, sir. Your suggestion worked brilliantly. We diverted the bus to a pre-arranged spot. They started shooting when they realised that they'd been rumbled but gave up when we brought in the big guns.' I was glad none of the British airmen had been hurt and strangely that the German infiltrators hadn't either. They would have been following orders in their own twisted way.

'Big guns?' Steve asked.

Ray turned to his men. 'I had an idea that disabling their bus in the open and having a Challenger tank roll up from the front, might take the fight out of them. Seems like I was right.'

'No woman then?' I wondered. 'She's the ring-leader.'

'No, ma'am. No sight of a woman. What does that mean, sir?'

His question was directed at Ray.

'It means, Wing Commander, that this base and all the visiting dignitaries are still in grave danger. That woman is an evil, conniving saboteur who is hell-bent on killing everyone here if she can.'

15

When we arrived at a large building on the edge of the airfield, Ray's men quickly deployed in all directions. There were already armed airmen gathered around but they seemed complacent, half-believing that the threat had been quashed. A few growled orders from the youthful Wing Commander saw them rapidly adopt a more wary stance.

Even in the dim light of the November evening, it was obvious that it was a hive of activity in the daytime, with what appeared to be new runways being constructed to one side. Two huge bulldozers were parked up next to a hydraulic scoop.

Being night time with no perceived threat from the Luftwaffe, the base was unlit and no planes were in the air. I wondered if Das Genie's influence had extended so high in the Nazi command machine that this solitude was to lull the base into a false sense of security so the attack from within would be more likely to proceed.

Ray and I were ushered inside to where a gathering of civilians and Generals, Field Marshals and someone I vaguely recognised from papers as the First Sea Lord were all talking, whilst partaking of a banquet.

A tall, lean man in his fifties was interrupted politely and led across to us. He had a plate of sandwiches in his hand.

'G'day. I gather that you're the young bloke we have to thank for warning us about them Ratzis. And this must be the Sheila that's been helping you. Reckon I owe you both a big thank you.'

There was no mistaking his accent; Aussie.

'Name's Bill.' He shook our hands.

'I recognise you,' I replied. 'My dad has a photo of you on his dartboard.'

He didn't miss a beat, maintaining

his broad smile. 'Just like my ex-wife, from what I understand. Do you share your father's opinion, Sister Newton?'

Bill had done his homework.

'I'm keeping an open mind, Bill. The fact that you're here, risking your own life, is commendable. Now, if you'll excuse us, the Sergeant and I need to find a woman in a truck with an 'X' of the side.'

'An 'X' . . . or a cross? I did notice a red cross truck drive by us, earlier this evening.'

His comment was so incisive, I wondered why the hell I hadn't seen it myself. Ray was on his walkie-talkie immediately.

Moments later one of his squad radioed back with a report of an ambulance parked about two hundred yards outside. The tyres had all been let down and the caller advised us that it seemed the rear of the truck was packed with explosives.

The Wing Commander asked about where it was.

'Next to the fuel tanks and fighter planes.' To have such a potentially dangerous situation in the midst of war was absolutely unbelievable. Clearly whoever was in charge here had a few kangaroos loose in the top paddock.

'Dear Lord.' His features paled at the thought. 'Those fuel lines run everywhere, even under this building. We need to evacuate everyone immediately.'

'Can't we move the truck away?' Ray asked. 'The explosives are probably on a timer.' 'Soggy ground. Flat tyres. If we could push it into the old quarry on the edge of the field, we might have a chance,' the Wing Commander yelled as he and Bill herded the panicked officials out of the building.

I stared out the open door towards the barely visible truck, where all the activity was focused. Someone was trying to push it with a jeep. It wasn't budging. Others were trying to move the fighter planes away.

'Didn't Archie say there'd be fireworks at eight o'clock?' Ray asked me.

'That's less than ten minutes. We'll never clear the base or save the planes in time.'

I grabbed the Commander by the shoulder. 'The bulldozers. Where are the keys?'

'Thought of that, lady. They're new technology. The construction workers have gone home. No one here can drive them.'

'I can,' I announced. 'Keys please.' My dad's business was diverse. Dozers were used a lot in Oz, not so much in Britain because of rain and mud.

'Pauline. It's too dangerous,' Ray pleaded but there was no choice. I grabbed the offered keys and began running, regretting for the dozenth time today not wearing more practical clothing. If I survived tonight a more sensible wardrobe was definitely on my Chrissie wish list, starting with those new-fangled trousers now being worn by women.

I clambered up onto the high seat, tearing my dress as I plopped down on the soaking wet seat. It was a drizzly rain. Ray clambered up beside me, covering my head with a sou'wester hat he tied under my chin.

The big engines screamed into life as I struggled to find the headlights switch. Ray shone a torch onto the complex panel. We started backwards.

'Damn. I was in reverse.'

Ray yelled in my ear over the roar of the huge beast 'You can drive this thing, can't you?'

'Been a while, Ray. There. First gear. Which way?'

'Left.'

'And where's the quarry?'

'I'll guide you, Pauline. Just get this thing moving faster. And get that blade positioned right. I don't want you tearing the top off the truck.'

'Lord, you're bossy. I hope you'll be kinder when we're married. Oh, I see the truck. Get everyone out of the way.'

'Where's the horn?'

I pointed and he pressed it repeatedly. People scattered as I eased the huge beast up to the rear of the Red Cross truck. The explosives were on a timer but I didn't want to push my luck. Ray hopped down to guide me. Once touching the rear of the 'ambulance', he climbed back up as we slowly started forward. The truck was in neutral with the handbrake off, but those flat tyres made it hard going. Someone up ahead was waving a torch to guide us the disused quarry chasm bordering the airfield.

'Can't you go any faster, Pauline?' Ray asked trying not to check his watch. 'Not that I'm putting any pressure on you, or anything.'

'This is not a racing car, my love. You get off. No point in both of us risking our lives.'

'No. We need to jam the accelerator down. We'll lose the dozer but that's the only way. We can both jump off.' He rummaged around, eventually finding a block of wood. The guy ahead ran back past us, shouting, 'I've left the torches on the cliff edge, about eighty yards off.' He vanished into the night behind us.

'No. The wood's not strong enough on the pedal. I'm going to have to push it over manually,' I declared, after a few feeble attempts. 'Ray! Get off.'

Ray jumped down but instead of running back, he guided me up to the quarry. I felt the trucks front wheels fall over the edge.

'Two more feet,' he yelled. Then the truck's own centre of gravity would pull it over. I could sense I was on the precipice, the torches now only just in front. I nudged the truck a little more but the clutch slipped and my machine jerked forward.

'Pauline!' Ray screamed.

'Sorry. Foot slipped.'

Just then, there was a grinding sound and the truck disappeared from view in slow motion. I stopped immediately but could sense the cliff edge moving under the weight of the dozer. Damn.

'Reverse. You need reverse, Pauline,' I told myself, in a real panic. 'You do not want to go forward.'

Slowly the treads gained traction and began to drag the behemoth of the machine backwards, inch by inch. The truck's resounding crash to the quarry floor was followed by a huge explosion that lit up the quarry and the sky ahead.

Hell. Was I still that close? I accelerated quicker now as the dull roaring in my ears diminished.

Ray clambered back up. 'Four minutes late. Good thing Germans don't make clocks.'

'The bomb was late?' I shuddered. The realisation that I'd almost died but for some incompetent bomb-maker scared the fur off me.

'You did it, Pauline. You saved us all.' He kissed me passionately wiping the rain from my cheeks with his own wet hands. He was right. The fact was that we were still alive. 'What ifs' didn't matter any longer.

'We did it, lover. Heaven knows how. Pity Sister Denmead wasn't in that truck.'

Taking our time, we trundled back towards the group of building lights in the dozer. However, a few hundred yards from the place where they'd all gone for sanctuary, the chatter of a machine gun began.

'You don't think . . . ?' Ray asked.

'Sister Denmead. One last attempt to cause chaos. She's a persistent little spy.'

'We need a distraction for my squad to subdue. How do you feel about driving straight into a hail of bullets?'

'Peachy!' I said, sarcastically. Out of the frying pan . . . 'Just let me position this blade though.' I worked the hydraulics until the blade of the bulldozer was high enough to protect us. The trouble was, it would stop us from seeing where we were heading also. Gunning the throaty engine, we charged forward. I switched all the forward lights on to try and blind Clara. Bullet-shells immediately flew over our head or pinged off the steel blades protecting us.

Then there were a few single shots

and a woman's cry of pain.

'We got her, boss,' a soldier announced, running up.

'Make certain she doesn't take a cyanide pill. I want her alive.'

It was over. Everyone was safe at last. Ray took me in his arms as we climbed down from the now stationary bull-dozer. I'd left the lights on.

'My heroine,' He said as we held each other. 'Good grief, Pauline. You're shaking. Must be the cold. Let's get you inside.'

It wasn't the cold. It was shock, yet Ray was kind enough not to press the issue. He helped me to walk towards the group of grateful people. I was shattered but at least my hair was dryish under the less than fashionable sou'wester.

Bill was one of the first to thank us as we were escorted inside. I must have looked a sight but I was too tired to care as they led me to a chair and covered me with a blanket.

'We make our women-folk strong

down under, Sister Newton. You're a credit to Australia. Is there anything I can do for you? Anything? Just name it.'

'Give us a minute please, Bill. But yes. There is something.' I scribbled some details with a pencil and sat back to close my eyes. Bill went off to make some hasty arrangements. As for me, I'd definitely had one of those days; my head was aching as was every part of my body. Driving that bulldozer was the hardest thing I'd ever had to do and the thought of dying if that huge bomb had detonated on time would give me nightmares for years to come.

And the day wasn't finished yet.

They gave me hot, sweet tea, food and a doctor gave me a check-over. Ray stayed with me, though injured himself. He left the processing of all the prisoners to others.

★   ★   ★

Finally, I felt rested enough to deal with my request to Bill. It wasn't huge in the grand scheme of things; just complicated. Ray and I were led through endless corridors to the radio room in the centre of the complex. It wasn't the one for talking to pilots. This was another which was far more secure.

Ever the politician, Bill took charge. 'Pauline. We'll have to use this microphone but everyone this end will hear what's being said at the other end over these speakers. It will be early morning there. Are you ready?'

I took a gulp of water and smiled at him and Ray. Ray took my hand. 'As I'll ever be.'

'Make the connection please,' Bill requested. There was a long delay and conversations with switchboard operators until we heard a ringing tone.

'Hello. This is Wagga Wagga 287.' It was Mum's voice, distorted a little but perfectly clear.

'Hello, Mrs Newton. This is Bill McKempster calling from England. I have someone who wishes to . . .'

I heard my dad interrupt. 'Give me

the phone, Miriam.' I heard Mum say who it was and a conversation about why would a big-wig like him be phoning Wagga. Dad came on at last.

'Hello?'

Bill tried a different tack. 'Mr Newton. Bill McKempster. Your daughter tells me you have my picture on your dartboard. She's with me now. We're both in England.'

'My daughter? Pauline?'

Bill handed me the mike. 'G'day, Dad. Just wanted to check you're all right after the op.'

'Crickey, Mum. It's Pauline. Come and listen in. Yeah, Pauline. Them docs fixed what was making me crook. I'm heaps better now. Hunky-dory.'

Unlike a normal phone call which was always rushed, Bill told us to take our time. We did. It was fantastic to catch up. I told them about now being a Sister and spoke to my little sis, Tilly.

Eventually, I introduced Ray. 'I've met this special bloke, Dad. Ray Tennyson. He has something he wishes to ask you.'

The silence was profound. 'Hello. Mr Newton. I realise you don't know me from Adam but I love your beautiful daughter and I'm asking for your permission to marry her.'

'Crikey, mate,' Dad exclaimed. 'You Poms don't beat around the bush, do you? What makes you reckon you're good enough?'

Ray was wondering how to respond. Bill jumped in. 'I realise I'm not your favourite politician, Mr Newton, but he and your daughter saved dozens of lives tonight, including mine. Ray's a ranking officer with the British Government. I can't say what rank but trust this old codger. He's a good'un.'

Dad had to agree after that ringing endorsement. Both he and Mum were overjoyed despite being upset that it might be a while before they met in person. We disconnected the call soon afterwards. I was dead on my feet.

Arrangements were made for us all to bed down on the base tonight. Ray promised me that he would continue to be based at Killymoor Hall. There was still the mole who leaked the meeting, to be caught. There was one final thing to do, though.

'Well?' I asked Ray. Everyone gathered around was also waiting. I felt bad asking him as he wasn't in the best of health. Glancing around, he couldn't very well back out.

Ray struggled but managed to get down on one knee. 'Pauline Newton. Will you do me the honour of marrying me?'

'Of course! Thought you'd never ask, soldier.' I helped him stand and we embraced, properly this time. Other details could wait but it would be great to set a date for our wedding. We looked at a calendar.

'Before Christmas,' I prompted.

Ray kissed me again.

'How about the seventh of December, nineteen forty-one, Pauline? It'll be a day to remember.'

Little did I realise how right he'd be.

NEW YEAR, NEW GUY

Angela Britnell

When Polly organises a surprise reunion for her fiancé and his long-lost American friend, her sister, Laura, grudgingly agrees to help keep the secret. And when the plain-spoken, larger-than-life Hunter McQueen steps off the bus in her rainy Devon town and only just squeezes into her tiny car, it confirms that Laura has made a big mistake in going along with her sister's crazy plan. But could the tall, handsome man with the Nashville drawl be just what Laura needs to shake up her life and start something new?

THE GHOST IN THE WINDOW

Cara Cooper

Working on a forthcoming movie, Siobhan Frost travels to a beautiful French chateau run by the charismatic Christian Lavelle. Having taken the job to escape her failed engagement, she is shocked when her ex, Gerrard, turns up. And when Philadelphia, the starlet appearing in the film, makes eyes at Gerrard, Siobhan is left in turmoil. One thing is for sure — the chateau has secrets and Christian is determined to solve them with Siobhan's help.